Terry Jones was born in1942 in Wales. He read English at
Oxford University and retains a passion for medieval history
and literature: his study of Chaucer's Knight received wide
c... ...o. He
b...... ...mber of
the Monty Python team. He co-directed *Monty Python and the
Holy Grail* and directed *Monty Python's Life of Brian*, *The
Meaning of Life* (which won the Grand Jury prize at Cannes
in 1983), *Eric the Viking*, *Personal Services* and *The Wind in the
Willows* (which won the Best Film in the International
Children's Film Festival in Chicago, 1998).

Terry Jones is married and lives in London.

Terry Jones

Fantastic Stories

Illustrated by Michael Foreman

PUFFIN BOOKS

PUFFIN BOOKS

Published by the Penguin Group
Penguin Books Ltd, 27 Wrights Lane, London W8 5TZ, England
Penguin Putnam Inc., 375 Hudson Street, New York, New York 10014, USA
Penguin Books Australia Ltd, Ringwood, Victoria, Australia
Penguin Books Canada Ltd, 10 Alcorn Avenue, Toronto, Ontario, Canada M4V 3B2
Penguin Books (NZ) Ltd, Private Bag 102902, NSMC, Auckland, New Zealand

On the World Wide Web at: www.penguin.com

Penguin Books Ltd, Registered Offices: Harmondsworth, Middlesex, England

First published by Pavilion Books Limited 1992
Published in Puffin Books 1994
This edition with black and white illustrations published 1995
13

Text copyright © Terry Jones, 1992
Illustrations copyright © Michael Foreman, 1992
All rights reserved

The moral right of the author and illustrator has been asserted

Set in 13/14 pt Monophoto Baskerville

Filmset by Datix International Limited, Bungay, Suffolk
Mad and printed in England by Clays Ltd, St Ives plc

British Library Cataloguing in Publication Data
A CIP catalogue record for this book is available from the British Library

ISBN 0-140-36279-7

For Tom Crowley
who heard most of these stories first

To the Reader

Although most of these stories could be called 'Fairy Tales' some of them don't fit that description, so I've named the book *Fantastic Stories*. Most of the tales were written between the end of November 1991 and the middle of January 1992, but two of them have appeared before. 'The Flying King' was first published in a collection of stories to mark the centenary of the National Society for the Prevention of Cruelty to Children: *Hundreds and Hundreds*, edited by Peter Dickinson (Puffin Books, 1984). 'Nicobobinus and the Doge of Venice' appeared in 'Puffin Post', Autumn 1987. If you want to know what happened to Nicobobinus and Rosie in the Land of Dragons, you'll have to read another book of mine called *Nicobobinus* (Pavilion Books, 1985, Puffin Books, 1987). I'd also like to thank my son, Bill Jones, for giving me the end of 'The Improving Mirror'.

Terry Jones

Contents

THE SHIP OF FOOLS

A young boy named Ben once ran away to sea. But the ship he joined was a very odd one indeed.

The Captain always wore his trousers tied over his head with seaweed. The Bosun danced the hornpipe all day long from dawn to dusk wearing nothing but beetroot juice. And the First Mate kept six families of mice down the neck of his jumper!

'This is a rum vessel, me hearty!' said Ben to one of the sailors, who was at that moment about to put his head into the ship's barrel of syrup.

'It's a Ship of Fools!' grinned the sailor, and he stuck his head in the syrup.

'I suppose you all must know what you're doing,' murmured young Ben, but the sailor couldn't reply because he was all stuck up with syrup.

Just then the Captain yelled: 'Raise the hanky! And sit on the snails!' Although, because he still had his trousers over his head, what it actually sounded like was: 'Gmpf der wmfky! Umf bmfwmf umf wmf!'

'I'm sure he means: "Raise the anchor! And set the sails!"' said young Ben to himself. But whatever it was the Captain had said, nobody seemed to be taking the slightest bit of notice.

'They must be doing more important things,' said Ben to himself. 'So I suppose *I'd* better obey Captain's orders.'

So Ben raised the anchor by himself, and hoisted the sails as best he could, and the ship sailed off into the blue.

'Where are we heading, shipmate?' Ben asked a sailor who was hanging over the side, trying to paint the ship with a turnip and a pot of lemonade.

'Goodness knows!' exclaimed the sailor. 'It's a Ship of Fools!'

'The Captain will know,' said Ben, and he climbed up to the bridge, where the Captain was standing upside-down at the wheel, trying to steer with his feet.

'I'm almost sure you shouldn't steer a ship like that,' said Ben to himself, 'but then what do I know? I'm just a raw land-lubber getting his first taste of the briney.' But even so, Ben realized that the Captain couldn't see where they were going, because his trousers were still over his eyes. As it happened, the ship was, at that moment, heading straight for a lighthouse! So Ben grabbed the wheel, and said: 'What's the course, skipper?'

'Bmf Bmf Wmf!' replied the Captain.

'Nor' Nor' West it is, sir!' said Ben, and he steered the ship safely round the lighthouse and off for the open sea.

Well, they hadn't sailed very far before a storm blew up.

'Shall I take in the yard-arm and reef the sails, Captain?' yelled Ben. But the Captain was far too busy trying to keep his game of marbles still, as the ship rolled from side to side.

The wind began to howl, and the sea grew angry.

'I better had, anyway,' said Ben to himself, and he ran about the ship, preparing for the storm ahead.

As he did so, the rest of the crew grinned and waved at him, but they all carried on doing whatever it was they were doing. One of them was hanging by his hair from the mainmast, trying to play the violin with a spoon. Another was varnishing his nose with the ship's varnish. While another was trying to stretch his ears by tying them to the capstan and jumping overboard.

'Well . . . I wouldn't have thought this was the way to run a ship!' said young Ben. 'I suppose they know the ropes and I'm just learning. Even so . . . I didn't realize the newest recruit had to do *everything*! But I suppose I'd better get on with it.' And he set about doing what he thought should be done, while the rest of the crew just grinned and waved at him.

The storm gathered force, and soon great waves

were lashing across the deck, as the ship rolled and wallowed. Ben rushed about trying to get everyone below decks, so he could batten down the hatches. But as soon as he got one sailor to go below another would pop up from somewhere else.

And all the time, the ship rolled, and before long it began to take on water.

'Cap'n! We must get the men below decks and batten down the hatches, while we ride out the storm!' yelled Ben.

But the Captain had decided to take his supper on the fo'c'sle, and was far too busy – trying to keep the waves off his lamb chop with an egg whisk – to listen to Ben.

And still the ship took on more water.

'She's beginning to list!' shouted Ben. 'The hold's filling with water!'

'It's OK!' said the Bosun, who had stopped doing the hornpipe, but was still only wearing beetroot juice. 'Look!' and he held up a large piece of wood.

'What's that?' gasped Ben.

'It's the ship's bung!' said the Bosun proudly. 'Now any water will run out through the bunghole in the bottom of the ship!'

'You're a fool!' yelled Ben.

'I know!' grinned the Bosun. 'It's a Ship of Fools!'

'Now we'll sink for sure!' cried Ben.

And, sure enough, the ship began to sink.

'Man the lifeboats!' yelled Ben. But the fools had all climbed up the mast and were now clinging to it, playing conkers and 'I Spy With My Little Eye'.

So Ben had to launch the lifeboat on his own. And he only managed to do it just as the ship finally went down. Then he had to paddle around in the terrible seas, fishing the crew of fools out of the heaving waters.

'I spy with my little eye something beginning with . . . S!' shouted the First Mate, as Ben hauled him into the lifeboat.

'Sea,' said Ben wearily, and rowed over to the next fool.

By the time night fell, Ben had managed to get the Captain and the Bosun and the First Mate and all the rest of the crew of fools into the little lifeboat. But they wouldn't keep still, and they kept shouting and laughing and falling overboard again, and Ben had his work cut out trying to keep them all together.

By dawn the storm had died down, and Ben was exhausted, but he'd managed to save everyone. One of the fools, however, had thrown all the oars overboard while Ben hadn't been watching, so they couldn't row anywhere. And now the First Mate was so hungry he'd started to eat the lifeboat!

'You can't eat wood!' yelled Ben.

'You can – if you're fool enough!' grinned the First Mate.

'But if you eat the lifeboat, we'll all drown!' gasped Ben.

'It's a pity we don't have a little pepper and salt,' remarked the Captain, who had also started to nibble the boat.

'It's salty enough as it is!' said the Bosun, who was tucking into the rudder.

'Urgh!' said the Chief Petty Officer. 'It's un-cooked! You shouldn't eat raw lifeboat!'

But they did.

By midday, they'd managed to eat most of the lifeboat, and Ben had just given them all up for lost, when, to his relief, he saw land on the horizon.

'Land ahead!' shouted Ben, and he tried to get the fools to paddle with their hands towards it, but they were feeling a bit sick from all the wood they'd just eaten. So Ben broke off the last plank and used that to paddle them towards the shore.

At last they landed, and the fools all jumped ashore and started filling their trousers with sand and banging their heads on the rocks, while young Ben looked for food.

He hadn't looked very far, when a man with a spear suddenly barred his way.

Ben tried to signal that he meant no harm, that he had been shipwrecked, and that he and his crew-mates were in sore distress. Once the man under-stood all this, he became very friendly, and offered Ben food and drink. But as soon as the two of them returned to Ben's shipmates, the crew of fools all leapt up making terrible faces and tried to chase the stranger off.

'Stop it!' cried Ben. 'He's trying to help us!' But the crew of fools had already jumped on the poor fellow, and started beating and punching him, until eventually he fled back to his village to fetch a war party.

7

'Now we can't even stay here!' screamed Ben. 'You're all fools!'

'Of course we are!' cried the Captain. 'We keep telling you – it's a Ship of Fools!'

Now I don't know how what happened next came about, or what would have happened to Ben if it hadn't, but it did. And this is what it was.

Young Ben was just wondering what on earth he was going to do, when a sail appeared on the horizon!

But before Ben could shout out: 'There's a ship!' he turned and saw the war party approaching with spears and bows and arrows, while the crew of fools were busy trying to bury the Bosun head-first in the sand.

Ben finally shook his head and said: 'Well, you've all certainly taught me one thing: and that's not to waste my time with those I can see are fools – no matter who they are – Captain, Bosun or First Mate!'

And with that, Ben dived into the sea and swam off to join the other boat. And he left the Ship of Fools to their own fate.

THE DRAGON ON THE ROOF

long time ago in a remote part of China, a dragon once flew down from the mountains and settled on the roof of the house of a rich merchant.

The merchant and his wife and family and servants were, of course, terrified out of their wits. They looked out of the windows and could see the shadows of the dragon's wings stretching out over the ground below them. And when they looked up, they could see his great yellow claws sticking into the roof above them.

'What are we going to do?' cried the merchant's wife.

'Perhaps it'll be gone in the morning,' said the merchant. 'Let's go to bed and hope.'

So they all went to bed and lay there shivering and shaking. And nobody slept a wink all night. They just lay there listening to the sound of the dragon's leathery wings beating on the walls behind their beds, and the scraping of the dragon's scaly belly on the tiles above their heads.

The next day, the dragon was still there, warming its tail on the chimney-pot. And no one in the house dared to stick so much as a finger out of doors.

'We can't go on like this!' cried the merchant's wife. 'Sometimes dragons stay like that for a thousand years!'

So once again they waited until nightfall, but this time the merchant and his family and servants crept out of the house as quiet as could be. They could hear the dragon snoring away high above them, and they could feel the warm breeze of his breath blowing down their necks, as they tiptoed across the lawns. By the time they got half-way across, they were so frightened that they all suddenly started to run. They ran out of the gardens and off into the night. And they didn't stop running until they'd reached the great city, where the king of that part of China lived.

The next day, the merchant went to the King's palace. Outside the gates was a huge crowd of beggars and poor people and ragged children, and the rich merchant had to fight his way through them.

'What d'you want?' demanded the palace guard.

'I want to see the King,' exclaimed the merchant.

'Buzz off!' said the guard.

'I don't want charity!' replied the merchant. 'I'm a rich man!'

'Oh, then in you go!' said the guard.

So the merchant entered the palace, and found the King playing Fiddlesticks with his Lord High Chancellor in the Council Chamber. The merchant fell on his face in front of the King, and cried: 'O Great King! Favourite Of His People! Help me! The Jade Dragon has flown down from the Jade Dragon Snow Mountain, and has alighted on my roof-top, O Most Beloved Ruler Of All China!'

The King (who was, in fact, extremely unpopular) paused for a moment in his game and looked at the merchant, and said: 'I don't particularly like your hat.'

So the merchant, of course, threw his hat out of the window, and said: 'O Monarch Esteemed By All His Subjects! Loved By All The World! Please assist me and my wretched family! The Jade Dragon has flown down from the Jade Dragon Snow Mountain, and is, at this very moment, sitting on my roof-top, and refuses to go away!'

The King turned again, and glared at the merchant, and said: 'Nor do I much care for your trousers.'

So the merchant, naturally, removed his trousers and threw them out of the window.

'Nor,' said the King, 'do I really approve of anything you are wearing.'

So, of course, the merchant took off all the rest of his clothes, and stood there stark naked in front of the King, feeling very embarrassed.

'*And* throw them out of the window!' said the King.

So the merchant threw them out of the window. At which point, the King burst out into the most unpleasant laughter. 'It must be your birthday!' he cried, 'because you're wearing your birthday suit!' and he collapsed on the floor helpless with mirth. (You can see why he wasn't a very popular king.)

Finally, however, the King pulled himself together and asked: 'Well, what do you want? You can't stand around here stark naked, you know!'

'Your Majesty!' cried the merchant. 'The Jade Dragon has flown down from the Jade Dragon Snow Mountain and is sitting on my roof-top!'

The King went a little green about the gills when he heard this, because nobody particularly likes having a dragon in their kingdom.

'Well, what do you expect me to do about it?' replied the King. 'Go and read it a bedtime story?'

'Oh no! Most Cherished Lord! Admired And Venerated Leader Of His People! No one would expect *you* to read bedtime stories to a dragon. But I was hoping you might find some way of . . . getting rid of it?'

'Is it a big dragon?' asked the King.

'It is. Very big,' replied the merchant.

'I was afraid it would be,' said the King. 'And have you tried asking it – politely – if it would mind leaving of its own accord?'

'First thing we did,' said the merchant.

'Well, in that case,' replied the King, '. . . tough luck!'

Just at that moment there was a terrible noise from outside the palace. 'Ah! It's here!' cried the King, leaping onto a chair. 'The dragon's come to get us!'

'No, no, no,' said the Lord High Chancellor. 'That is nothing to be worried about. It is merely the poor people of your kingdom groaning at your gates, because they have not enough to eat.'

'Miserable wretches!' cried the King. 'Have them all beaten and sent home.'

'Er . . . many of them have no homes to go to,' replied the Chancellor.

'Well then – obviously – just have them beaten!' exclaimed the King. 'And sent somewhere else to groan.'

But just then there was an even louder roar from outside the palace gates.

'*That's* the dragon!' exclaimed the King, hiding in a cupboard.

'No,' said the Chancellor, 'that is merely the rest of your subjects demanding that you resign the crown.'

At this point, the King sat on his throne and burst into tears. 'Why does nobody like me?' he cried.

'Er . . . may I go and put some clothes on?' asked the merchant.

'Oh! Go and jump out of the window!' replied

the King.

Well, the merchant was just going to jump out of the window (because, of course, in those days, whenever a king told you to do something, you always did it) when the Lord High Chancellor stopped him and turned to the King and whispered: 'Your Majesty! It may be that this fellow's dragon could be just what we need!'

'Don't talk piffle,' snapped the King. '*Nobody* needs a dragon!'

'On the contrary,' replied the Chancellor, '*you* need one right now. Nothing, you know, makes a king more popular with his people than getting rid of a dragon for them.'

'You're right!' exclaimed the King.

So there and then he sent for the Most Famous Dragon-Slayer In The Land, and had it announced that a terrible dragon had flown down from the Jade Dragon Snow Mountain and was threatening their kingdom.

Naturally everyone immediately forgot about being hungry or discontented. They fled from the palace gates and hid themselves away in dark corners for fear of the dragon.

Some days later, the Most Famous Dragon-Slayer In The Whole Of China arrived. The King ordered a fabulous banquet in his honour. But the Dragon-Slayer said: 'I never eat so much as a nut, nor drink so much as a thimbleful, until I have seen my dragon, and know what it is I have to do.'

So the merchant took the Dragon-Slayer to his house, and they hid in an apricot tree to observe the dragon.

'Well? What d'you think of it?' asked the merchant.

But the Dragon-Slayer said not a word.

'Big, isn't it?' said the merchant.

But the Dragon-Slayer remained silent. He just sat there in the apricot tree, watching the dragon.

'How are you going to kill it?' inquired the merchant eagerly.

But the Dragon-Slayer didn't reply. He climbed down out of the apricot tree, and returned to the palace. There he ordered a plate of eels and mint, and he drank a cup of wine.

When he had finished, the King looked at him anxiously and said: 'Well? What are you going to do?'

The Dragon-Slayer wiped his mouth and said: 'Nothing.'

'Nothing?' exclaimed the King. 'Is this dragon so big you're frightened of it?'

'I've killed bigger ones,' replied the Dragon-Slayer, rubbing his chest.

'Is it such a fierce dragon you're scared it'll finish you off?' cried the King.

'I've dispatched hundreds of fiercer ones,' yawned the Dragon-Slayer.

'Then has it hotter breath?' demanded the King. 'Or sharper claws? Or bigger jaws? Or what?'

But the Dragon-Slayer merely shut his eyes and

said: 'Like me, it's old and tired. It has come down from the mountains to die in the East. It's merely resting on that roof-top. It'll do no harm, and, in a week or so, it will go on its way to the place where dragons go to die.'

Then the Dragon-Slayer rolled himself up in his cloak and went to sleep by the fire.

But the King was furious.

'This is no good!' he whispered to the Lord High Chancellor. 'It's not going to make me more popular if I leave this dragon sitting on that man's roof-top. It needs to be killed!'

'I agree,' replied the Lord High Chancellor. 'There's nothing like a little dragon-slaying to get the people on to your side.'

So the King sent for the Second Most Famous Dragon-Slayer In The Whole Of China, and said: 'Listen! I want you to kill that dragon, and I won't pay you unless you do!'

So the Second Most Famous Dragon-Slayer In The Whole Of China went to the merchant's house and hid in the apricot tree to observe the dragon. Then he came back to the palace, and ordered a plate of pork and beans, drank a flask of wine, and said to the King: 'It's a messy business killing dragons. The fire from their nostrils burns the countryside, and their blood poisons the land so that nothing will grow for a hundred years. And when you cut them open, the smoke from their bellies covers the sky and blots out the sun.'

But the King said: 'I want that dragon killed. Mess or no mess!'

But the Second Most Famous Dragon-Slayer In The Whole Of China replied: 'Best to leave this one alone. It's old and on its way to die in the East.'

Whereupon the King stamped his foot, and sent for the Third Most Famous Dragon-Slayer In The Whole Of China, and said: 'Kill me that dragon!'

Now the Third Most Famous Dragon-Slayer In The Whole Of China also happened to be the most cunning, and he knew just why it was the King was so keen to have the dragon killed. He also knew that if he killed the dragon, he himself would become the First Dragon-Slayer In The Whole Of China instead of only the Third. So he said to the King: 'Nothing easier, Your Majesty. I'll kill that dragon straightaway.'

Well, he went to the merchant's house, climbed the apricot tree and looked down at the dragon. He could see it was an old one and weary of life, and he congratulated himself on his good luck. But he told the King to have it announced in the market square that the dragon was young and fierce and very dangerous, and that everyone should keep well out of the way until after the battle was over.

When they heard this, of course, the people were even more frightened, and they hurried back to their hiding places and shut their windows and bolted their doors.

Then the Dragon-Slayer shouted down from the apricot tree: 'Wake up, Jade Dragon! For I have come to kill you!'

The Jade Dragon opened a weary eye and said: 'Leave me alone, Dragon-Slayer. I am old and weary of life. I have come down from the Jade Dragon Snow Mountain to die in the East. Why should you kill me?'

'Enough!' cried the Dragon-Slayer. 'If you do not want me to kill you, fly away and never come back.'

The Jade Dragon opened its other weary eye and looked at the Dragon-Slayer. 'Dragon-Slayer! You know I am too weary to fly any further. I have settled here to rest. I shall do no one any harm. Let me be.'

But the Dragon-Slayer didn't reply. He took his bow and he took two arrows, and he let one arrow fly, and it pierced the Jade Dragon in the right eye. The old creature roared in pain, and tried to raise itself up on its legs, but it was too old and weak, and it fell down again on top of the house, crushing one of the walls beneath its weight.

Then the Dragon-Slayer fired his second arrow, and it pierced the Jade Dragon in the left eye, and the old creature roared again and a sheet of fire shot out from its nostrils and set fire to the apricot tree.

But the Dragon-Slayer had leapt out of the tree and on to the back of the blinded beast, as it struggled to its feet, breathing flames through its nostrils and setting fire to the countryside all around.

It flapped its old, leathery wings, trying to fly away, but the Dragon-Slayer was hanging on to the spines on its back, and he drove his long sword deep into the dragon's side. And the Jade Dragon howled, and its claws ripped off the roof of the merchant's house, as it rolled over on its side and its blood gushed out on to the ground.

And everywhere the dragon's blood touched the earth, the plants turned black and withered away.

Then the Dragon-Slayer took his long sword and cut open the old dragon's fiery belly, and a black cloud shot up into the sky and covered the sun.

When the people looked out of their hiding places, they thought the night had fallen, the sky was so black. All around the city they could see the countryside burning, and the air stank with the smell of the dragon's blood. But the King ordered a great banquet to be held in the palace that night, and he paid the Dragon-Slayer half the money he had in his treasury.

And when the people heard that the dragon

had been killed, they cheered and clapped and praised the King because he had saved them from the dragon.

When the merchant and his wife and children returned to their house, however, they found it was just a pile of rubble, and their beautiful lawns and gardens were burnt beyond repair.

And the sun did not shine again in that land all that summer, because of the smoke from the dragon's belly. What is worse, nothing would grow in that kingdom for a hundred years, because the land had been poisoned by the dragon's blood.

But the odd thing is, that although the people were now poorer than they ever had been, and scarcely ever had enough to eat or saw the sun, every time the King went out they cheered him and clapped him and called him: 'King Chong The Dragon-Slayer', and he was, from that time on, the most popular ruler in the whole of China for as long as he reigned and long after.

And the Third Most Famous Dragon-Slayer In The Whole Of China became the First, and people never tired of telling and retelling the story of his fearful fight with the Jade Dragon from the Jade Dragon Snow Mountain.

What do you think of that?

The Star of the Farmyard

There was once a dog who could perform the most amazing tricks. It could stand on its head and bark the Dog's Chorus whilst juggling eight balls on its hind paws and playing the violin with its front paws. That was just one of its tricks.

Another trick it could do was this: it would bite its own tail, then it would roll around the farmyard like a wheel, balancing two long poles on its paws – on top of one of which it was balancing Daisy the Cow and on the other Old Lob the Carthorse – all the while, at the same time, telling excruciatingly funny jokes that it made up on the spot.

One day Charlemagne, the cock, said to Stanislav the dog: 'Stan, you're wasted doing your amazing tricks here in this old farmyard – you ought to go to the Big City or join the circus.'

Stan replied: 'Maybe you're right, Charlemagne.'

So one bright spring morning, Stanislav the Dog and Charlemagne the Cock set off down the road to seek their fortunes in the Big City.

They hadn't gone very far before they came to a fair. There were people selling everything you could imagine. There was also a stage on which a troupe of strolling players were performing.

So Charlemagne the Cock strode up to the leader of the troupe and said: 'Now, my good man, this is indeed your lucky day, for you see before you the most talented, most amazing juggler, acrobat, ventriloquist, comedian and all-round entertainer in the whole history of our – or any other – farmyard ... Stanislav the Dog!' And Stanislav who all this time had been looking modestly down at his paws, now gave a low bow.

'Can't you read?' said the leader of the troupe. 'No dogs!'

And without more ado, Charlemagne the Cock and Stanislav the Dog were thrown out.

'Huh!' said Charlemagne, picking himself up and shaking the road-dust out of his feathers. 'You're too good for a troupe of strolling players anyway.'

Stanislav climbed wearily out of the ditch. He was covered in mud, and he looked at his friend very miserably.

'I'm tired,' he said. And I want to go home to my master.'

'Cheer up, my friend!' replied Charlemagne the Cock. 'We're going to the Big City, where fine ladies and gentlemen drip with diamonds, where dukes and earls sport rubies and emeralds, and where the streets are paved with gold. With your talents, you'll take 'em by storm. We'll make our fortunes!'

So the cock and the dog set off once more down the long, dirty road that led to the Big City.

On the way they happened to pass a circus. Charlemagne the Cock strode up to the ringmaster, who was in the middle of teaching the lions to stand on their hind legs and jump through a ring.

'Tut! tut! tut! my good man,' said Charlemagne the Cock. 'You needn't bother yourself with this sort of rubbish any more! Allow me to introduce you to the most superlative acrobat and tumbler – who can not only stand on his hind paws, but can jump through fifty such rings . . . backwards and whilst balancing one of your lions on his nose . . . and do it all on the high wire . . . *without a safety net*!'

'I only do tricks with lions,' said the ringmaster.

'But Stanislav the Dog has more talent in his right hind leg than your entire troupe of lions!'

'These are the best lions in the business!' exclaimed the ringmaster. 'And they'd eat you and your dog for supper without even blinking. In fact they need a feed right now!' And he reached out his hand to grab Charlemagne the Cock. Stan the Dog saw what was happening, however, and nipped the ringmaster on the ankle.

'Run, Charlemagne!' he yelled.

And Charlemagne ran as fast as he could, while Stan the Dog leapt about – nipping people's ankles

– as the entire circus chased them down the road.

'Help!' squawked Charlemagne, as the circus folk got closer and closer and hands reached out to grab him by the neck.

But Stan the Dog ran under everyone's legs and tripped them up. Then he said to Charlemagne: 'Jump on my back! I can run four times as fast as these clowns!'

And so they escaped, with Charlemagne the Cock riding on Stan the Dog's back.

That night they slept under a hedge. Charlemagne the Cock was extremely nervous, but Stan the Dog curled himself around his friend to protect him. Stan himself, however, was not very happy either.

'I'm hungry,' he murmured, 'and I want to go home to my master.'

'Cheer up!' said Charlemagne. 'Tomorrow we'll reach the Great City, where your talents will be appreciated. Forget these country yokels. I'm telling you – fame and fortune await you and . . .'

But his friend was fast asleep.

Well, the next day, they arrived in the Great City. At first they were overawed by the noise and bustle. Many a time they had to leap into the gutter to avoid a cart or a carriage, and on one occasion they both got drenched when somebody emptied a chamber-pot from a window above the street, and it went right over them.

'Oh dear, I miss the farmyard,' said Stan the

Dog. 'And nobody here wants to know us.'

'Brace up!' cried Charlemagne. 'We're about to make our breakthrough! We're going straight to the top!' And he knocked on the door of the Archbishop's palace.

Now it so happened that the Archbishop himself was, at that very moment, in the hallway preparing to leave the palace, and so, when the servant opened the door, the Archbishop saw the cock and the dog standing there on the step.

'Your Highness!' said Charlemagne, bowing low to the servant. 'Allow me to introduce to you the Most Amazing Prodigy Of All Time – Stanislav the Dog! He does tricks you or I would have thought impossible! They are, indeed, miracles of . . .'

'Clear off!' said the servant, who had been too astonished to speak for a moment. And he began to close the door.

But Charlemagne the Cock suddenly lost his temper.

'LISTEN TO ME!' he cried, and he flew at the servant with his spurs flying. Well, the servant was so surprised he fell over backwards, and Charlemagne the Cock landed on his chest and screamed: 'THIS DOG IS A GENIUS! HIS LIKE HAS NEVER BEEN SEEN OUTSIDE OUR FARMYARD! JUST GIVE HIM A CHANCE TO SHOW YOU!'

And Stan the Dog, who had nervously slunk into the hallway, started to do his trick where he bounced around on his tail, juggling precious china ornaments (which he grabbed off the sideboard as he bounced past) whilst barking a popular Farmyard Chorus that always used to go down particularly well with the pigs.

'My china!' screamed the Archbishop. 'Stop him at once!' And several of the Archbishop's servants threw themselves at Stan the Dog. But Stan bounced out of their way brilliantly, and grabbed the Archbishop's mitre and started to balance a rare old Ming vase on the top of it.

'Isn't he great?' shouted Charlemagne the Cock.

'Grab him!' screamed the Archbishop, and the servants grabbed Charlemagne.

'But look at the dog!' squawked the cock. 'Don't you see how great he is? Do you know anyone else who can juggle like that?'

But just then – as luck would have it – all the butlers and chambermaids and kitchen skivvies and gardeners, who had heard all the noise, came

28

bursting into the Archbishop's hall. They stood there for a moment horrified, as they watched a barking dog, bouncing around on his tail, juggling the most precious pieces of the Archbishop's prize collection of china.

'Stop him!' roared the Archbishop again. And without more ado everybody descended on poor Stan, and he disappeared under a mound of flailing arms and legs. As a result, of course, all the Archbishop's best china crashed to the floor and was smashed into smithereens.

'Now look what you've done!' yelled Charlemagne.

'Now look what *we've* done!' exclaimed the Archbishop. 'Listen to me! You're both filthy, you look as if you slept in a hedge, you stink of the chamber-pot and you dare to burst into my palace and wreck my best china! Well! You're going to pay for it! Throw them into my darkest dungeons!'

And the Archbishop's servants were just about to do so, when suddenly a voice spoke from above them.

'Silence, everybody!' said the Voice.

Everybody froze. Then the Voice continued: 'Don't you know who this is? Archbishop! Shame on you! This is the Voice of God!'

The Archbishop fell to his knees, and muttered a prayer, and everyone else followed suit.

'That's better!' said the Voice of God. 'Now let Stan the Dog go free. He didn't mean no harm.'

So they let go of Stan the Dog.

'And now,' continued the Voice of God. 'Let Charlemagne the Cock go!'

So they let go of Charlemagne the Cock.

'Now shut your eyes and wait for me to tell you to open them again!' said the Voice of God.

So they all shut their eyes, and Stan the Dog and Charlemagne the Cock fled out of the Archbishop's palace as fast as their legs could carry them.

I don't know how long the Archbishop and his servants remained kneeling there with their eyes shut, but I am certain that the Voice of God never told them to open their eyes again. For, of course, the Voice wasn't the Voice of God at all – it was the Voice of Stan the Dog.

'You are, as I say, a very talented dog,' said Charlemagne as they ran down the road. 'But I'd almost forgotten you were a ventriloquist as well!'

'Luckily for us!' replied Stan. 'But look here, Charlemagne, I'll always be talented – it's just the way I am. Only I'd rather use those talents where they're appreciated, instead of where they get us into trouble.'

'Stanislav,' said Charlemagne, 'maybe you're right.'

And so the two friends returned to the farmyard. And Stanislav the Dog continued to perform his astounding tricks for the entertainment of the other farm animals, and they always loved him.

And even though Charlemagne occasionally

squawked a bit at night, and said that it was a waste of talent, Stan the Dog stayed where he was – happy to be the Star of the Farmyard.

THE IMPROVING MIRROR

A magician once made a magical mirror that made everything look better than it really was.

It would make an ugly man look handsome, and a plain woman beautiful.

'I will bring happiness to a lot of people with this mirror,' said the Magician to himself. And he went to the main city, where he had his invention announced to the public. Naturally everybody was very curious to see themselves more handsome and more beautiful than they really were, and they queued up to see the magical improving mirror.

The Magician rubbed his hands and said: 'I will not only make people happy – I will also make my fortune!'

But before he was able to show the mirror to a single person, a most unlucky thing occurred.

It so happened that the King of that particular

country had married a Queen who was bad-tempered, selfish and cruel. The King put up with all her faults of character, however, because she was also very, very beautiful. She also happened to be extremely vain. So when she heard about the improving mirror, she simply couldn't wait to get her hands on it before anyone else.

'But, my dear,' said the King, 'you know you are already the most beautiful lady in the realm. And I should know – I searched the kingdom through and I found no one whose looks surpassed yours. That's why I married you.'

But the Queen replied: 'I must see how even more beautiful I can look in this magical mirror.' And nothing would satisfy her but to be the first to look in the improving mirror.

So the King sent for the Magician with strict instructions that he was to show the mirror to nobody until he had demonstrated it to Queen Pavona.

Well, the Magician entered the audience chamber with a feeling of dread.

'Great Queen!' he said with a low bow. 'You are the most peerless beauty in this land. No one could be more beautiful than you are now. I beg you not to look in my magic mirror!'

But the Queen could not contain her eagerness to see herself in the improving glass, and she said: 'Show me at once! I must see myself even more beautiful than I really am!'

'Alas!' said the Magician. 'I made this mirror

for those less fortunate in looks – to give them hope of how they might be.'

'Show me!' cried Queen Pavona. 'Or I will have you executed on the spot!'

Well, the poor Magician saw there was nothing for it but that he must show the Queen the magic improving mirror. So he brought out the special box in which he kept it locked away, but he did so with a heavy heart.

He took the key, which he had tied around his waist, and opened up the lock. The courtiers pressed around, but the King ordered them to stand back, and the box was brought nearer the throne.

Then the Magician lifted the lid, and the Queen peered in. There she saw the magic mirror – lying face down.

'Your Majesty!' said the Magician. 'I fear only evil will come of your looking in my magic mirror.'

'Silence!' shouted the Queen, and she seized the mirror and held it up to her face.

For some moments she did not speak, nor move, nor even breathe. She was so dazzled by the reflection before her. If her eyes had been dark and mysterious before, now they were two pools of midnight. If her cheeks had been fair and rosy before, now they were like snow touched by the dawn sun. And if her face had been well-shaped before, now it was so perfect that it would carry away the soul of anyone who gazed upon it.

For what seemed a lifetime, her eyes feasted on

34

the image before her. And everyone in the court waited with bated breath.

Eventually the King spoke: 'Well, my dear? what do you see?' he asked.

Slowly the Queen came to her senses. As she did so, the Magician trembled in his shoes, and humbled himself on the floor before her.

'Does it make you more beautiful?' asked the King.

Queen Pavona suddenly hid the mirror in her sleeve, glared around the court and cried: 'Of course not! It's just an ordinary mirror! Have this charlatan thrown into the darkest dungeon!'

So the poor Magician was carried off down to the darkest dungeon.

Meanwhile the King turned to Queen Pavona and said: 'Perhaps it will work for me, since I am less well-favoured than you.'

'I tell you it's just an ordinary mirror!' cried the Queen. 'I shall use it in my chamber.'

36

And with that, she went straight to her room, and hid the magic mirror in her great chest.

Now the truth of the matter is that the moment Queen Pavona had looked into the magic mirror and seen herself even more beautiful than she really was, she had been consumed with jealousy. She could not bear the thought that there was a beauty greater than hers – even though it was that of her own reflection! So she locked the mirror away, resolving that no one should ever look in it again.

None the less, she could not forget what she had seen in that looking-glass, and – despite her resolve – she found herself drawn to it, and time and again she would creep into her room and steal a look in the magic glass. Before long, she was spending many hours of the day alone in her chamber, gazing into that mirror, trying to see what made her reflection so much more beautiful than she already was.

As the weeks passed, Queen Pavona began to try and make herself more like her reflection in the magic looking-glass. But, of course, it was no use. For no matter how beautiful she made herself, her reflection became even more beautiful still.

The more she tried, the more she failed, and the more she failed to be as beautiful as her reflection in the magic mirror, the more time she spent alone in her room, gazing into it. Until eventually she hardly ever came out of her room – not even to eat or to dance or to make merry with the rest of the court.

Meanwhile the King grew more and more anxious about his wife, for she never explained to him what kept her in her room from morn till night, and whenever he entered the chamber, she always took care to hide the magic mirror.

One night, however, after Queen Pavona had been poring all day over her reflection in the fatal looking-glass, she fell asleep with it still in her hand.

It so happened that some time later the King entered her chamber to kiss her goodnight, as was his custom.

The King had, long ago, guessed that the magic mirror was the cause of his wife's strange behaviour, and he too had long been curious to see just what was so special about it. So when he found her fast asleep on her couch, with the magic mirror still in her hand, he couldn't resist. He lifted it slowly to her face and gazed into it. And there he saw for the first time his Queen's reflection in the magic looking-glass.

The King had believed he would never find another woman more beautiful to his sight than Queen Pavona. But now he saw in the magic mirror the reflection of someone who was three times as beautiful, and he let out a cry as if he had been stabbed to the heart.

At that, the Queen woke up with a scream of rage, and she struck the King with the mirror – so hard that he fell over.

'How dare you look in this mirror!' she cried, her face all screwed up with anger. Well, of course, when the King looked at her now with her face distorted by rage, he thought that Queen Pavona was almost ugly compared to her reflection.

'How dare you strike me!' cried the King. And he strode out of the Queen's chamber, resolving that he would put up with her ill-temper no longer.

From that day on, the King scarcely spoke to his Queen, or even set eyes on her. But he could not forget the vision of loveliness that he had seen in the magic glass.

Now all this while, the poor Magician had been languishing in the darkest dungeon. And every day he cursed himself for making the improving mirror.

Then one day, in the midst of his misery, the door of his cell was flung open and in strode the King!

The Magician fell at his feet and cried: 'Mercy, O King! Have you come to release me? You know I've done nothing wrong.'

'Well . . . that's as maybe,' replied the King. 'But if you want to get out of this dungeon, there is something you must do for me.'

'Anything that is within my power!' exclaimed the Magician.

'Very well,' said the King. 'I want you to change the Queen, my wife, for her reflection in your magic looking-glass.'

'But, Your Majesty!' cried the Magician. 'That would be a cruel thing to do to your wife!'

'I don't care!' replied the King. 'I am sick of her evil temper, her selfishness and her cruelty. And now I have seen her reflection – which is so much more beautiful than she ever can be – I am no longer even satisfied by her looks. Can you change her for her reflection?'

'Alas!' cried the Magician. 'Is this the only way I can gain my freedom?'

'If you can't do it, then you can rot in here until you die – for all I care!' said the King.

'Then I shall do it,' said the Magician. 'But we shall both suffer for it.'

And so the King released the Magician from his dungeon, and the Magician was led into the Queen's chamber.

The Queen was standing as usual in front of the magic glass, staring at her reflection. 'What do you want?' she cried as the King entered.

'You wish you were more like your reflection, my dear?' said the King. 'Then so do I!'

At which the Magician threw a handful of magic dust into the air, and for a few moments it filled the chamber so that no one could see. Then, as the dust cleared, a most extraordinary thing happened.

There was a flash and a groan, and suddenly the mirror rose up into the air – but the Queen's reflection stayed where it was! Then the mirror turned over several times in the air, before landing over the Queen herself.

And so the King had his wish.

From that time on, Queen Pavona's beautiful reflection became his wife, and the real queen was trapped for ever in the mirror. But, just as the Magician had promised, the King lived to regret the change. For even though she was now his wife, the Queen's reflection was still only a reflection, and – when the King tried to touch her beautiful skin – he found it was as cold as glass.

What's more, he soon discovered that the Queen's reflection was not only more beautiful than the real Queen, it was also more heartless, more selfish and even more ill-tempered. And many a time he longed for the Magician to change them back.

But the Magician had long since fled the country, and now lived in miserable exile, swearing that he would never make another magic mirror that could so inflame the vanity of those who were already vain enough.

The Mermaid Who Pitied a Sailor

There was once a mermaid who pitied the sailors who drowned in the windy sea.

Her sisters would laugh whenever a ship foundered and sank, and they would swim down to steal the silver combs and golden goblets from the sunken vessels. But Varina, the mermaid, wept in her watery cave, thinking of the men who had lost their lives.

'What in the sea is the matter with you?' her sisters would exclaim. 'While we are finding jewels and silver, you sit alone and grieve. It's not our fault if their ships are wrecked! That is the way the sea goes. Besides, these sailors mean nothing to us, sister, for they are not of our kind.'

But Varina the mermaid replied: 'What though they are not of our kind? Their hopes are still hopes. Their lives are lives.'

And her sisters just laughed at her, and splashed her with their finny tails.

One day, however, a great ship struck the rocks near by and started to sink. All the other mermaids stayed sitting on the rocks where they had been singing, but Varina slipped away into the sea, and swam around and around the sinking ship, calling out to see if any sailors were still alive.

She saw the Boatswain in his chair, but he had drowned as the ship first took water. She saw the First Mate on the poop deck, but he had drowned, caught in the rigging. She saw the Captain, but he, too, was lifeless, with his hands around the wheel.

Then she heard a tap-tap-tapping, coming from the side of the sunken ship, and there was the frightened face of the Cabin Boy, peering through a crack.

'How are you still alive, when your ship-mates are all drowned?' asked Varina.

'I'm caught in a pocket of air,' replied the Cabin Boy. 'But it will not last, and we are now so deep at the bottom of the ocean, that unless I can swim as fast as a fish through the ship's hold, through the galley and up on to the deck, I shall drown long before I can make my way up to the waves above.'

'But I swim faster than forty fishes!' exclaimed the mermaid. And without more ado, she twitched her tail, and swam to the deck, and down through the galley and along through the ship's hold to the place where the Cabin Boy was trapped in the pocket of air.

Then she took his hand and said: 'Hold your

landlubberly breath!' And back she swam, faster than forty fishes, back through the ship's hold, back through the galley and up to the deck and then up and up and up to the waves above.

There the Cabin Boy got back his breath. But the moment he turned to the mermaid, it left his body again, for he suddenly saw how beautiful she was.

'Thank you!' he finally managed to say. 'Now I can swim to the shore.' But the mermaid would not let go of his hand.

'Come with me to my watery cave,' she said.

'Oh no!' cried the Cabin Boy. 'You have saved my life, and grateful I am more than six times seven, but I know you mermaids are not of our kind and bring us poor sailors only despair.'

But still the mermaid would not let go of his hand, and she swam as fast as forty fishes, back to her watery cave.

And there she gave the Cabin Boy sea-kelp and sargassum, bladder-wrack and sea-urchins, all served up on a silver dish. But the Cabin Boy looked pale as death and said:

'Your kindness overwhelms me, and grateful I am more than six times sixty, but you are not of my kind, and these ocean foods to me are thin and savourless. Let me go.'

But the mermaid wrapped him up in a seaweed bed and said: 'Sleep and tomorrow you may feel better.'

The Cabin Boy replied: 'You are kind beyond words, and grateful I am more than six times six

hundred, but I am not of your kind, and this bed is cold and damp, and my blood runs as chill as sea-water in my veins.'

Finally the mermaid said to the Cabin Boy: 'Shut your eyes, and I shall sing you a song that will make you forget your sorrow.'

But at that, the Cabin Boy leapt out of the bed and cried: 'Oh no! That you must not! For don't you know it is your mermaids' singing that lulls our senses and lures us poor sailors on to the rocks so that we founder and drown?'

When the mermaid heard this, she was truly astonished. She swam to her sisters and cried out: 'Sisters! Throw away those silver combs and throw away those golden goblets that we have stolen from the drowned sailors – for it is our songs that lull these sailors' senses and lure them on to the rocks.'

When they heard this, the mermaids all wept salty tears for the lives of the men who had been drowned through their songs. And from that day on the mermaids resolved to sit on the rocks and sing only when they were sure there was no ship in sight.

As for Varina, she swam back to her watery cave, and there she found the Cabin Boy still waiting for her.

'I could not leave,' he said taking her hand. 'For though we are of different kind, where shall I find such goodness of heart as yours?'

And there and then he took the mermaid in his

arms and kissed her, and she wrapped her finny tail around him, and they both fell into the sea.

Then they swam as if they were one creature instead of two – fast as forty fishes – until, at last, they reached the land the Cabin Boy had left, many years before. And there they fell asleep upon the shore – exhausted and sea-worn.

When the Cabin Boy awoke, he looked and he found Varina still asleep beside him. And as he stared at her, all the breath once again went from his body, for her finny tail had disappeared, and there she lay beside him – no longer a mermaid, but a beautiful girl, who opened her eyes and looked at him not with pity but with love.

FORGET-ME-NUTS

A long, long time ago in a very distant land, there once lived a king with a very bad conscience. But he didn't let his conscience trouble him one little bit, because in that land there also happened to grow a very rare and peculiar fruit. It was known as the forget-me-nut. And whenever King Yorick felt bad about something he'd done, or something he hadn't done, he would chew a forget-me-nut, and whatever it was that was worrying him would simply vanish from his mind.

One cold winter's day, for example, King Yorick was being carried home to his palace in his specially heated chair, when he noticed a poor man dressed in rags with his wife and three small children shivering under a wall.

'Oh dear,' said King Yorick, when he got back to his palace. 'I really ought to do something about all the poor people who have nowhere to live in this bitter cold weather. I suppose I ought to convert one of my palaces into a home for them . . .'

'Oh! But, Your Majesty!' said his Chancellor. 'You've only got sixteen palaces! If you were to lose one of them, you'd have one less than King Fancypants of Swaggerland – and that wouldn't do, would it?'

'Good gracious no! That wouldn't do at all,' replied King Yorick.

'Best go to bed and chew one of those delightful forget-me-nuts,' said his Chancellor.

'Yes, perhaps you're right,' sighed King Yorick.

So he put himself to bed with a hot-water bottle, chewed a forget-me-nut, and had soon forgotten all about the poor family, who were freezing outside in the ice and snow.

But, of course, the poor man and his family outside didn't have any forget-me-nuts to chew on. Forget-me-nuts were worth their weight in gold – far too rare and expensive for the likes of them.

And even if they could have found one, it wouldn't have done them any good, for, you see, forget-me-nuts only helped you to forget your conscience – they didn't help you to forget that you were cold or hungry or homeless.

As a matter of fact, the forget-me-nuts didn't really help King Yorick that much either, for even though he chewed on one most days – and sometimes two or three – he was always pretty miserable, though he never quite knew why.

'Perhaps if I had another palace built so I had

one *more* than King Fancypants of Swaggerland –
I'd feel happier?' said King Yorick.

'Exactly so,' said the Lord Chancellor (whose
brother got all the building contracts).

And so King Yorick had yet another palace built.
It was opened with great celebrations and fantastic
fireworks and a lavish feast that went on for three
whole days. Then the new palace stood empty for
the rest of the year like all the other palaces.

Now the poor man, whose family the King had seen
shivering in the midst of winter, had a son whose
name was Tim. And one day, Tim said to his
father: 'Father! I cannot bear to see you so unhappy!
I'm going to bring King Yorick to his senses!'

Whereupon Tim's father exclaimed: 'But what
on earth can you do, Tim? You're so small.'

'You'll see!' said Tim. And there and then he
set off for the King's palace.

When he reached it, he found the doors shut
tight against the freezing winter and the walls too
high to climb.

'What *am* I going to do?' thought Tim to himself. 'I'll never even get into the palace – let alone
bring the King to his senses!'

But he didn't give up. He sat on a stone outside
the palace and waited to see what would happen.
And as he sat there, the sky grew dark and the
world grew quiet, as if it too were waiting to see
what would happen. Then finally it started to
snow. And the snow fell on Tim's head and

shoulders. But still he just sat there, watching the King's palace.

Well, after a while, Tim saw a face at one of the windows. And all the while the snow fell thicker and faster, until it quite covered Tim's head and his shoulders. Yet still Tim just sat and waited to see what would happen.

Before long, the window opened, and a boy stuck his head out and called to Tim: 'Aren't you cold?'

Now Tim was so used to being cold that he scarcely thought about it any more. But, now he came to think about it, he realized he was so cold he couldn't even speak.

'You'd better come in and get warm,' said the boy at the window.

But Tim found he could neither speak nor move. He was frozen fast and completely covered in snow like a snowman.

So the boy climbed out of the window, brushed the snow off Tim, and lifted him in through the window. (For, truth to tell, Tim was extremely small and light because he'd never really had enough to eat all his life.)

Well, it didn't take Tim long to thaw out and explain what he was doing.

'That's odd!' replied the boy. 'I was wondering what I could do to make *my* father happier too.'

'But your father's the king!' exclaimed Tim, who had already guessed that the boy was King Yorick's son. 'He must have everything he could ever want!'

'That's right,' replied the Prince. 'But he's miserable from morn till night. I try and cheer him up, but he doesn't even seem to notice I exist. He just sits and chews forget-me-nuts.'

When Tim heard this, he sat and stared into the fire.

'How on earth are we going to help our fathers to be happier?' he said.

No sooner had he spoken these words than a most extraordinary thing happened. The fire began to move, and, as the two boys watched, the red-hot coals turned over and around until they formed themselves into a face that spoke and said: 'The Key of Memory is the only thing that will bring your fathers happiness. But be warned – it will also bring grief as well.'

'Where do we find the Key of Memory?' asked Tim.

'Go with your consciences . . .' replied the fire.

'What?' said the Prince.

'What?' said Tim.

But the coals in the fire shifted around again, and didn't say another word.

Then suddenly there was a noise like thunder. Tim and the Prince rushed to the window and looked out into the freezing black night. They could see two points of light coming towards them fast.

'What d'you think they are?' asked Tim.

'Perhaps they're our consciences,' said the Prince.

'Don't be daft!' said Tim.

And the two points of light got nearer and nearer, until suddenly two huge black stallions, breathing fire out of their nostrils, burst out of the night, leapt over the palace wall, and reared up to a halt underneath the window.

Tim looked at the Prince, and the Prince looked at Tim, and Tim shrugged and said: 'Well, I don't know . . . maybe you're right . . .' And without another word they leapt on to the backs of those stallions and galloped off into the night.

The next morning, when King Yorick found that his son had vanished, he wrung his hands in despair. 'What shall I do? My only son has run away . . . I should have loved him more! I should have been a better father!'

'Don't make such a fuss!' said his Chancellor. 'Just chew a forget-me-nut, and you'll soon feel better.'

So the King ate a forget-me-nut, and, after a while, he forgot all about it. But when he went to bed that night, he found the Queen crying into her pillow.

'What on earth's the matter with you?' he asked.

The Queen looked at him in anger and exclaimed: 'What! Have you already forgotten that our son has run away?'

'Oh, don't make such a fuss,' said the King. 'Have a forget-me-nut.' And he offered the bowl of nuts to the Queen, but she seized it from his grasp and threw the entire thing on the fire.

'Don't!' cried the King. 'Those are worth their weight in gold!' But it was too late. The nuts burst into flame, and the smoke went up the chimney.

Meanwhile, Tim and the Prince were riding through the frozen Northlands on the backs of their fire-breathing stallions.

By and by, they saw a cloud on the horizon, and the stallions redoubled their speed. And, by and by, they reached the cloud and found it was a pall of smoke, under which their stallions came to a halt. When Tim and the Prince looked down, they saw they were on the edge of a sheer cliff that dropped straight down a thousand feet into a lake of fire.

But they didn't have time to be frightened, for – to their horror – their stallions reared up, pawed the air, and then leapt straight off the cliff and plunged down towards the fiery lake.

The two boys shut their eyes, convinced that their last moment had come, but, as they reached the surface of the burning lake and they felt the fire licking up around their stallions' bellies, suddenly the flames seemed to separate, and they found themselves plummeting down into a black hole until they disappeared below the surface of the lake of fire.

For a moment, their eyes were filled with smoke, and they couldn't see a thing, but when they opened them again, they found they had landed in a vast cavern. And there in the centre of the cavern was a great forge, with flames shooting up and feeding the fiery lake above. At the forge worked a huge blacksmith, with iron bands on his arms and fire coming from his nostrils.

The two stallions reared in the air once more, and Tim and the Prince fell off onto a pile of straw.

When he saw them, the huge blacksmith stopped his work and laughed. And every time he laughed, the flames shot out from his nostrils and set fire to his beard, so he had to keep running to the water-butt to put it out.

Meanwhile Tim had got to his feet and said:

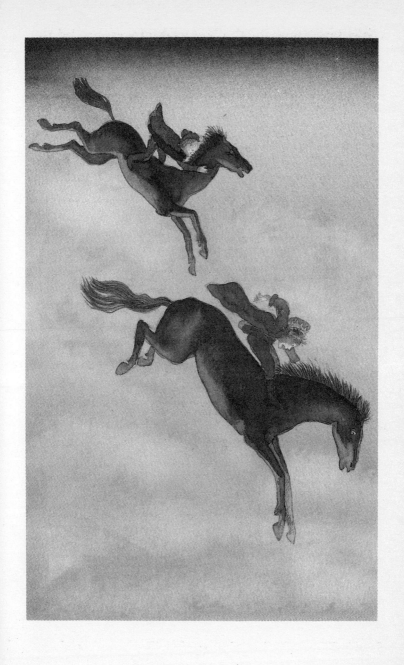

'We have come for the Key of Memory.'

'Have you now?' roared the blacksmith, and this time he laughed so hard that he set fire to his hood, and he had to plunge his whole head into the water-butt.

'We've been told it is the only thing that will bring our fathers happiness,' said the Prince.

'And grief!' roared the blacksmith, and he laughed again so long and loud that he set fire to his jerkin, and he had to jump into the water-butt right up to his neck.

'Is the Key of Memory here?' asked Tim.

The blacksmith lay there, half in the water, and roared: 'I've just finished making it! It's on the anvil.'

The two boys turned and saw a huge key lying on the anvil and glowing red-hot.

'Take a pair of tongs,' said the blacksmith, 'and drop it in this water butt.'

So the Prince took a long pair of tongs, lifted up the red-hot key and dropped it into the water-butt, where the giant blacksmith was still sitting. Immediately the blacksmith disappeared in a cloud of steam, and when the steam had cleared away, the blacksmith had gone, and there was an old woman, whose face was red like the coals of the fire. The old woman turned to the Prince and said:

'Prince! In the unhappiest part of your father's kingdom, you will find a chest filled with your father's memories. This is the only key that will unlock it.'

Then the old woman seemed to fall into pieces,

58

and sank like glowing embers down into the water-butt.

So Tim and the Prince took the key, and looked for their black stallions, but they had disappeared too.

'Well,' said Tim. 'It looks as if we've got to walk home.'

The two boys searched until eventually they found the entrance to the cavern, and they were able to climb up and escape. When they reached the world above, however, they found that the lake of fire was just an ordinary lake. And there at the water's edge were two grey horses – just ordinary horses.

They rode back through the frozen Northlands, but what had taken a few minutes on the marvellous stallions now took days. And what had taken hours now took weeks.

But eventually they arrived back in the land of King Yorick.

'Where shall we find the unhappiest part of my father's kingdom?' asked the Prince.

'I know where that is!' said Tim, and he led the Prince to the place where forty beggars slept under a bridge, but they couldn't find the chest there.

Then Tim led the Prince to a shed, where twenty robbers were hiding for fear of being caught. But they didn't find the chest there.

Finally Tim led the Prince to the place where his own mother and father and brother and sister were huddled around a poor fire, beneath the wall. But when they saw Tim, their faces burst into smiles of happiness, and they didn't find the chest there.

'Well, it beats me,' said Tim. 'I don't know where else to look.'

So the Prince returned to the palace, and Tim went with him. There they found the King sitting under a nutmeg tree with tears in his eyes.

The Prince stood in front of his father, and said: 'What is the matter? You're the King! You have seventeen palaces and everything your heart could desire! Why are you unhappy?'

The King looked at his son without recognizing him and said: 'I forgot to love my son, and he ran away. And now I've even forgotten what he looks like!'

At that moment, Tim noticed that the King was sitting on a rusty old iron chest. He handed the key to the Prince and the Prince tried it in the lock. It fitted exactly.

'Father,' said the Prince. 'I've come back in hopes to bring you happiness.'

With that, he unlocked the chest, and at once the lid flew open and a million black thoughts flew into the air and blotted out the sun for a moment.

The King gave a roar of grief, as the black cloud suddenly melted into his mind, and he looked into the Prince's eyes and said:

'My son, I fear this is not happiness you have brought me, for I now remember everyone who has gone hungry – even for a day. I now remember every poor mother who cannot feed her children.

I now remember every poor father who cannot clothe his family nor provide a roof to keep the rain and snow from their heads. I now remember everyone whose sufferings I have ignored, and my heart is overcome with grief.'

'But, Your Majesty!' cried Tim. 'Why don't you give up just one of your seventeen palaces to house the hungry?'

King Yorick looked at Tim and, for the first time in years, he smiled: 'I'll do better than that!' he said.

And then and there King Yorick became the first king to give up living in a palace. Instead he lived in a comfortable house, that was just roomy enough for himself and his family and also for Tim and his mother and father and brother and sister. King Yorick opened up every one of his seventeen palaces so that from that day on there was not one single homeless person in the kingdom.

The Lord Chancellor left in disgust, and went to work with King Fancypants of Swaggerland. And so did the Chancellor's brother.

Then King Yorick ordered his gardeners to cut down all the orchards of forget-me-nut trees. This they did. And from that day on everyone forgot that there was ever such a thing as a forget-me-nut.

EYES-ALL-OVER

There was once an old man whose name was Eyes-All-Over, because that's what he had. He had eyes in the back of his head, eyes on the top of his head, eyes on his elbows, and eyes on his knees. He even had one eye on the bottom of each foot.

'Nobody ever catches me out!' chuckled old Eyes-All-Over. And it was true, because each of his eyes could see different things.

The eyes in the back of his head could see things that happened yesterday. The eyes on the top of his head could see things that happened a long way away. The eyes on his elbows could see everyone else's mistakes. The eyes on his knees could see everyone else's hopes. And the eyes on the soles of his feet could see things that would never happen.

Now the only thing in the whole world that old

Eyes-All-Over really cared for was a pot of gold that he kept under the floorboards in his bedroom. Every night he would close all the shutters, draw the curtains, take out his pot of gold and count it – just to make sure it was all there.

And as he counted it, the eyes on the top of his head looked around to make sure no one was peeping in – while the eyes in the back of his head made sure the coins were the same as they were yesterday.

Every week his pot of gold would get larger, because, whenever he went to market, the eyes in his elbows spotted everyone else's mistakes – so, if someone were selling a pig for a pound that was really worth three, old Eyes-All-Over would snap it up and sell it again as quick as fat in the frying-pan!

And, of course, old Eyes-All-Over never warned anybody they were making a mistake or that they'd lose their money. Oh no! He was far too busy thinking about adding all those golden guineas to his pot of gold.

Well, one day, Eyes-All-Over was sitting at home, counting through his pot of gold as usual, when suddenly there was a knock on the door.

'Burglars!' he exclaimed to himself. Then he thought: 'No ... wait a minute ... burglars wouldn't knock on the door. They'd just climb down the chimney.'

So he carefully hid away his pot of gold, and then he opened the door – just a crack.

There on the step stood a thin girl who said: 'I'm hungry and I have nowhere to live. May I do some work for you to earn a slice of bread and dripping?'

'Bread and dripping!' exclaimed old Eyes-All-Over. 'D'you think I'm made of money?'

'I could clean your house or chop your wood for you,' said the girl.

'Listen!' said Eyes-All-Over. 'The eyes in my knees can see what you're hoping – you're hoping to be rich one day and live in a nice house like this! Why, you'd probably cut my throat while I'm asleep! Be off with you!'

'Oh no!' said the poor girl. 'I'd never do a thing like that!'

Well, old Eyes-All-Over slyly slipped off a shoe and looked at the girl with one of the eyes in the soles of his feet – the eyes that could see things that would never happen. He saw at once that she would never do anything to harm anyone.

'Hmm! Very well,' he said. 'I do need some firewood chopping.'

So the girl chopped some firewood, and he gave her a piece of bread (without any dripping) and let her sleep that night in the woodshed.

The next day, old Eyes-All-Over woke up to find his house clean and neat and a breakfast of beans and ham waiting for him on the table. For the girl (whose name was May) had been up working hard for several hours already.

So Eyes-All-Over gave her another piece of dry bread and said: 'You can stay another day.'

Well, May stayed and worked for old Eyes-All-Over for some years. In return he let her sleep in the woodshed and allowed her to eat one piece of bread in the morning and one bowl of soup at night. 'Eh, eh!' he used to grin to himself. 'She costs me nothing and she works as hard as six men. What a bargain!'

One day, however, a stranger was riding past the house, when he caught sight of May digging the cabbage patch. She was still dressed in the same rags she'd been wearing when she first arrived (for it never occurred to old Eyes-All-Over that she might need new clothes) and she was exhausted from all her hard work, but even so May looked so beautiful that the young man fell in love with her on the spot. And, not long after, she fell in love with him.

So the young man went to Eyes-All-Over and told him that he wanted to marry May.

Now old Eyes-All-Over saw at once that he must be a rich young fellow. 'Eh, eh!' he thought, 'I can make a good bargain out of this business!'

But he put on a sad face and said: 'Oh no! You can't take young May away from me! She cooks my breakfast every morning!'

'Very well,' said the young man, 'take this.' And he handed old Eyes-All-Over a ruby ring. 'With that you can hire the finest cook in the world to make your breakfast every day!'

But old Eyes-All-Over slyly looked at the young man with the eyes in the back of his head – the eyes that could see things that had happened

65

yesterday – and he could see that only yesterday the young man had bought a fine fur coat. So old Eyes-All-Over screwed up his face and looked very sad and said: 'Oh, young sir, you don't really mean to take young May away from me? Don't you know she cuts my wood every day and makes my fire . . . I'd need a fine fur coat to keep me warm, if you were to take her away from me.'

So the young man went and fetched the fine fur coat, which he had actually bought for his father, and gave it to old Eyes-All-Over.

'There,' he said. 'Now may I marry May?'

But old Eyes-All-Over looked with the eyes on the top of his head – the eyes that could see things that were happening far away – and he could see that the young man's father, who was waiting for his return, lived in a fine palace, surrounded by fabulous wealth.

So Eyes-All-Over took out his hanky, and pretended to cry salty tears into it.

'Oh, good sir!' he said. 'You cannot possibly want to take young May away from me! She works so hard and keeps my house so neat and clean. Why! She's worth her weight in gold!'

So the young man rode off and returned, some time later, with a chest filled with gold pieces that altogether weighed exactly the same as young May.

'Now,' he said, 'May and I must go and be married.'

But old Eyes-All-Over hadn't finished yet. 'I can still screw even more out of this bargain!' he said to himself. Then he looked at the young man with the eyes in his knees – the eyes that could see people's hopes – and he could see that the young man had hopes, one day, to be a king – for he was, in fact, a prince.

So old Eyes-All-Over clutched his heart and said: 'Ah! Good sir! Would you take this child from me? She has been like a daughter to me these many years. I would not part with her for half a kingdom!'

'Very well,' said the Prince, and there and then he signed away half his kingdom to old Eyes-All-Over. Then he lifted May up on to his horse, and they rode off together – to be married with great feasting and merry-making in his father's palace.

As they rode away, old Eyes-All-Over rubbed his hands with glee.

'What a bargain!' he said to himself. 'I get all those years of work out of that thin stick of a girl, and then I sell her off for jewels and furs and gold and half a kingdom! I certainly am the sharpest chap around!'

But, at that very moment, he looked at himself with the eyes in his elbows – the eyes that saw people's mistakes – and he saw, to his horror, that he himself had made a big mistake, though he didn't know what.

As he got his lonely breakfast, however, and sat by his lonely fire, he began to realize what it was, for he found himself longing to hear May's voice singing in the garden and to see her face across the room. Soon he found himself thinking that he would give back everything just to have May give him one of her smiles.

But, when he looked at himself with the eyes in the soles of his feet – the eyes that saw things that would never happen – he knew she would never smile at him again.

And this time, old Eyes-All-Over cried real tears, for he suddenly realized that – when he gave May away – he'd given away the only thing he'd ever really loved.

And he cursed himself that – all the time she'd lived with him – he'd given her nothing but hard words and hard work, and had never given her any reason to care for him.

And old Eyes-All-Over then saw – clearer than anything he'd ever seen in his life – that despite having eyes all over, he had really been quite, quite blind.

An old woman once wished she had a child. But she never married, and now she lived all alone in a bare cottage beside a dark wood.

One day, however, around Christmas time, when the sky was yellow and heavy with snow, she looked out of the little window by her bed, and thought she saw the evening star.

'That's strange,' she said to herself, 'to see the evening star on such a stormy night. It must be a lucky star.'

So there and then she made a wish. I can't tell you what she wished for, because she never told anyone, but I think I can guess – can't you?

Now, as it happened, the light that the old woman had seen was not the evening star – in fact it was not a star at all, but a firefly. The firefly overheard the old lady's wish, and felt very sorry for her. So it flew to the place where all fireflies go to fetch their lights, and told its comrades what it had heard. And they all agreed to try and help her.

Well that night it began to snow from the black sky on to the black ground, until – as if by magic – the ground turned white, and the morning broke over a different world.

The old woman woke up and put on her shawl. Then she took a shovel and cleared away the snow from her door.

When she looked at the pile of snow she'd made, she smiled to herself and said: 'I don't think the evening star has granted my wish – so I'll make myself my own baby.'

And she spent the morning making the pile of snow into a snow baby.

That night, she sat in her cottage and felt very lonely. So she went to the door, and looked out at her snow baby.

'Tomorrow is Christmas Day,' she said to her snow baby. 'And here am I all alone in the world, and nobody cares whether I'm alive or dead – except you. And you'll be gone when the snows thaw.'

Then she climbed into her bed, and put out her candle.

A moment later she woke up and looked out of her window. She could hear a sound like tiny bells jingling far, far away, and she could see a strange yellow light all around her cottage. She could not see, but above her all the fireflies in the world were gathered together on her roof. The last one had just arrived, and now they all flew together to form one single ball of light.

The next moment, the old woman couldn't
believe her eyes as she watched a glowing ball
of light descend on to the heap of snow that

she had shaped like a baby. The light landed where the baby's heart would be. Then it poured into the snow baby and filled it top to toe!

The instant it did, the snow baby opened its eyes and looked around.

'What are you doing out there in the cold?' said the old woman. 'Come in at once.'

So the snow baby stepped unsteadily down from its little mound, and toddled towards the cottage door.

The old woman rushed to the door, flung it open and lifted her snow baby up in her arms. She kissed it and held it tight.

'Now,' she said, 'I will not be alone this Christmas.'

Then she tucked the snow baby up in her own bed, and bustled about the cottage to make everything ready.

The next morning the snow baby awoke to find a stocking hanging at the end of the bed.

'You must look in your stocking and see what St Nicholas has brought you,' said the old woman.

So the snow baby opened its stocking. Inside there was a chocolate medal, a wooden man on a trapeze, an old doll with one eye missing, a mince pie and an apple in the toe.

When the snow baby had opened all its presents and played with its toys, the old woman said: 'Now we must have our breakfast.'

So she sat her snow child on the other side of

73

the table, and they both ate a little toast and drank a little warm milk.

Just then they heard the church bell sounding across the snow. 'Now,' said the old woman, 'it's time we went to church.'

So she dressed the snow baby up in a woollen hat and muffler and a knitted woollen coat, and off they went, through the snow to the little church on the hill.

No one noticed the old woman and her snow baby, as they slipped into the back of the church while everyone else was on their knees. The two of them sat close together in the very back pew, holding hands. When the moment came, they stood up and sang the carols. Then, before the end of the service, they stole out again, before anyone else saw them.

Then the old woman and her snow baby ran back through the snow, laughing and shouting and throwing snowballs at each other.

When they finally got back to the cottage, there was a good smell coming from the old woman's oven.

'Now we must eat our Christmas pudding and mince pies,' said the old woman. 'I'm afraid I haven't got a goose or a ham pie to offer you.'

But the snow baby didn't seem to mind at all. They both sat down and ate the happiest Christmas dinner that the old woman could remember since she was a child.

As they finished, night began to fall, and the snow

74

baby grew tired, and the light with which it was filled grew dimmer – for the truth is that the fireflies needed to fetch new lights.

The old woman looked rather sadly at her snow baby.

'Must you go?' she asked. And the snow baby nodded. 'Well, thank you for keeping me company this Christmas,' said the old woman. 'I wish it could have gone on longer ... but there it is ...'

And then the first wonderful thing happened. The snow baby got up from its chair and came across to the old woman and kissed her.

And then the second wonderful thing happened. It spoke. 'Goodbye,' it said. Then it went out of the door, and the old woman watched from her window, as the snow baby climbed back on to its little mound of snow. Then the fireflies came out, one by one, and flew off dimly into the night to fetch new lights.

And the old woman fell asleep, nodding to herself as she remembered all the things she'd done that Christmas Day with her snow baby.

The next day, the sun shone, and the snows had gone. The old woman lit a fire and bustled about her little cottage. And when she felt brave enough, she went out of her door, and swept away the last heap of snow that had been – for a short time – her very own snow baby.

In the great long-ago, the badger was pure white all over.

'How sorry I feel for the Bear with his dull brown coat,' the Badger would say. 'And who would want to be like Leopard – all covered in spots? Or – worse still – like Tiger, with his vulgar striped coat! I am glad that the Maker Of All Things gave me this pure white coat without a blemish on it!'

This is how the Badger would boast as he paraded through the forest, until all the other creatures were thoroughly sick and tired of him.

'He always looks down his nose at me,' said the Rabbit, 'because only my tail is white.'

'And he sneers at me,' said the Field Mouse, 'because I'm such a mousy colour.'

'And he calls me an eye-sore!' exclaimed the Zebra.

'It's time we put a stop to it,' they said.

'Then may I make a suggestion?' asked the Fox, and he outlined a plan to which all the other animals agreed.

Some time later, the Fox went to the Badger and said:

'O Badger, please help us! You are, without doubt, the best-looking creature in the Wild Wood. It's not just your coat (which is exceedingly beautiful and without a blemish) but it is also . . . oh . . . the way you walk on your hind legs . . . the way you hold your head up . . . your superb manners and graceful ways . . . Won't you help us humbler animals by giving us lessons in how to improve our looks and how to carry ourselves?'

Well, the Badger was thrilled to hear all these compliments and he replied very graciously: 'Of course, my dear Fox. I'll see what I can do.'

So the Fox called all the animals to meet in the Great Glade, and said to them: 'Badger, here, has kindly agreed to give us lessons in how to look as handsome as he does. He will also instruct us in etiquette, deportment and fashion.'

There were one or two sniggers amongst the smaller animals at this point, but the Badger didn't notice. He stood up on his hind legs, puffed himself up with pride, and said: 'I am very happy to be in a position to help you less fortunate animals, and I must say I can see much room for improvement. You, Wolf, for example, have such a shabby coat . . .'

'But it's the only one I've got!' said the Wolf.

'And I pity you, Beaver,' went on the Badger,

'such an ordinary pelt you have . . . and as for that ridiculous tail . . .'

'Er, Badger,' interrupted the Fox, 'rather than going through all our short-comings (interesting and instructive though that certainly may be), why don't you teach us how to walk with our noses in the air – the way that makes you look so distinguished and sets off your beautiful un-blemished white coat so well?'

'By all means,' said the Badger.

'Why not walk to the other end of the Glade, so we can see?' said the Fox.

'Certainly,' said the Badger. And so, without suspecting a thing, he started to walk to the other end of the Glade.

Now if the Badger had not been so blinded by his own self-satisfaction, he might have noticed the Rat and the Stoat and the Weasel smirking behind their paws. And if he had looked a little closer, he might have noticed a twinkle in many an animal's eye. But he didn't. He just swaggered along on his hind legs with his nose right up in the air, saying:

'This is the way to walk . . . notice how grace-fully I raise my back legs . . . and see how I am always careful to keep my brush well oooooooooaaaarrrgggggghhhup!'

This is the moment that the Badger discovered the Fox's plan. The Fox had got all the other animals to dig a deep pit at one end of the Great Glade. This they had filled with muddy water and madder-root, and then covered it over with branches and fern.

The Badger, with his nose in the air, had, of course, walked straight into it – feet first. And he sank in – right up to his neck.

'Help!' he cried. 'Help! My beautiful white coat! Please pull me out someone! Help!'

Well, of course, all the animals in the Glade laughed and pointed at the poor Badger, as he struggled to keep his head out of the muck. Eventually he had to pull himself out by his own efforts.

When the Badger looked down at his beautiful white coat, stained with mud and madder-root, he was so mortified that he ran off out of the forest with a pitiful howl. And he ran and he ran until he came to a lake of crystal water.

There he tried to clean the stuff off his coat, but madder-root is a powerful dye, and no matter what he did, he could not get it off.

'What shall I do?' he moaned to himself. 'My beautiful white coat ... my pride and joy ... ruined for ever! How can I hold my head up in the forest again?'

To make matters worse, at that moment, a creature whom the Badger had never seen before swam up to him and said: 'What are you doing – washing your filthy old coat in our crystal-clear lake? Push off!'

The badger was speechless – not only because he wasn't used to being spoken to like this, but also because the creature had such a beautiful coat. It was as white and unblemished as the Badger's own coat used to be.

'Who are you?' asked the Badger.

'I'm Swan of course,' replied the Swan. 'Now shove off! We don't want dirty creatures like you around here!' And the Swan rose up on its legs and beat its powerful wings, and the Badger slunk away on all fours, with his tail between his legs.

For the rest of that day, the Badger hid himself away in a grove overlooking the crystal lake. From there he gazed down at the white Swan, gliding proudly about the lake, and the Badger was so filled with bitterness and envy that he thought he would burst.

That very night, however, he stole down to the Swan's nest, when the Swan was fast asleep, and very, very gently, he pulled out one of the Swan's feathers and then scuttled back to his hiding-place.

He did the same thing the next night, and the next and the next, and each night he returned to the grove, where he was busy making himself a new coat of white feathers, to cover up his stained fur.

And, because the Badger did all this so slowly and slyly, the Swan never noticed, until all but one of his feathers had disappeared.

That night the Swan couldn't sleep, because of the draught from where his feathers were missing, and so it was that he saw the Badger creeping up to steal the last one. As he did so the Swan rose up with a terrible cry. He pecked off the Badger's tail and beat him with his wings and chased him off.

Then the Swan returned to the crystal lake, and sat there lamenting over his lost feathers.

When the Maker Of All Things found the Swan – that he had made so beautiful – sitting there bald and featherless, he was extremely surprised.

But he was even more surprised when he went to the Wild Wood, and found the Badger parading about, looking quite ridiculous in his stolen feather coat!

'Badger!' exclaimed the Maker Of All Things. 'I knew you were vain, but I didn't know you were a thief as well!'

And there and then he took the feathers and gave them back to the Swan.

'From this day on,' he said to the Badger, 'you will wear only your coat stained with madder-root. And, if you're going to steal, I'd better give you a thief's mask as well!'

And the Maker Of All Things drew his fingers across the Badger's eyes, and left him with two black stripes – like a mask – from ears to snout.

The Badger was so ashamed that he ran off and hid, and to this very day all badgers avoid company. They live in solitude, stealing a little bit here and there, wherever they can. And each and every badger still wears a mask of stripes across its eyes.

OLD MAN TRY-BY-NIGHT

Old Man Try-By-Night prowls round the house after dark. He rattles a window here, and he bangs a door there – just to see if anyone's left one open. And, if anyone has, this is what he does.

Old Man Try-By-Night slips right in and makes himself at home. He spreads marmalade on the doormat, puts his dirty feet up on the kitchen table, and has a little snack.

He doesn't eat all the doormat – in fact you'd scarcely notice he's been at it – he just nibbles a little bit here and a little bit there. Then he takes out the sugar bowl and empties just a little sugar into his smelly old trousers so they crackle when he sits. He likes that. Then Old Man Try-By-Night pads around, putting his dirty fingers here and making muddy footmarks there. Then, once he's quite satisfied that everybody is fast asleep, do you know what he does? He slips right out again, and bangs the door so that everyone wakes up!

Oh yes! And there's something else that he does, but I can never remember what it is . . .

Well, one night, a small boy named Tom was lying in bed, when he thought he could hear Old Man Try-By-Night rattling the doors and windows downstairs.

'He's not going to keep me awake!' said Tom, and he jumped out of bed and crept downstairs.

Now, nobody has ever seen Old Man Try-By-Night, because he doesn't like to be seen in his dirty old galoshes and his old torn overcoat. So he always makes himself scarce as soon as anyone stirs.

But young Tom was known to be the quietest boy in his school. He was always very, very quiet. And tonight, creeping downstairs to try and catch Old Man Try-By-Night, Tom was quieter than he'd ever been ever before in his life.

Well, he was so quiet that not even Old Man Try-By-Night, with his sharp ears, heard him.

Tom stood as still as a chimney, peering round the kitchen door. He could see Old Man Try-By-Night peering in at the kitchen window, and he saw him grin and give it just a little rattle. Then he watched as Old Man Try-By-Night tried the back-door handle. He rattled it once. He rattled it twice. Then he looked up to see if he'd woken anybody up yet, but nobody seemed to be stirring. And young Tom just stood in the shadows, still as stone.

Old Man Try-By-Night gave a chuckle, and turned the door handle, and – to Tom's horror – it opened! His mother must have forgotten to lock the back door!

Tom's heart jumped into his throat, as he watched Old Man Try-By-Night slip through the door and stand there in the kitchen – large as life – looking around with that chuckly grin still on his face, and a big, dirty red handkerchief hanging from his overcoat pocket.

Before Tom could take another breath, Old Man Try-By-Night was padding across the floor towards him! For a moment, Tom thought he'd been spotted and that Old Man Try-By-Night was going to come and grab him with his grimy hands, and tie that filthy old red hanky round his eyes to stop him watching. But the Old Man hadn't even so much as noticed a whisper of Tom – he was simply padding over to the broom that stood in the corner. Old Man Try-By-Night looked at the dirty bristles and licked his lips. Then he padded round to the pantry and opened a jar of chocolate-spread in his grimy fingers. Next he stuck the dirty broom into it and got a good dollop of chocolate on the bristles. Then he sat down, put his filthy old galoshes up on the kitchen table, and started to nibble on the broom.

And he only stopped in order to wipe his chocolatey mouth on his filthy sleeve.

All this time, Tom stood there, peering round the kitchen door, as still and as silent as the clock on the kitchen wall that had stopped nine years

ago – before Tom was born.

But Tom said to himself: 'That's too much! It's one thing to keep us awake at night rattling the windows and doors, but nibbling my mother's best broom is really downright rude!'

So Tom suddenly stepped into the kitchen and said: 'Hey! Old Man Try-By-Night! Stop that!'

Well, of course, Old Man Try-By-Night leaps to his feet and drops the broom and bangs his head on the cupboard that Tom's father always bangs his head on and keeps meaning to move.

'Ow!' shouts Old Man Try-By-Night, and he makes for the back door as fast as his muddy old galoshes can take him. But Tom gets there first, and he locks it and throws the key into the sink.

'Oh! Please let me out!' whimpers Old Man Try-By-Night. 'I'm only doing a bit of broom-nibbling!'

But young Tom stands his ground and says: 'Now listen here, Old Man Try-By-Night! I'm fed up with your keeping me awake at night, rattling doors and windows. If I let you out of here, you must promise me you'll stop it.'

'I promise,' says Old Man Try-By-Night. 'But just unlock the door and let me out, for I hate being seen in my dirty old galoshes and my old torn overcoat.'

'Very well,' says young Tom. 'But look at the mess you've made of the kitchen. You've put your grimy fingermarks on the pantry door, you've got mud-marks on the kitchen table, and you've got chocolate on the broom! Before I let you out, you must clean it all up!'

'Very well,' sighs Old Man Try-By-Night, and he gets out his dirty old red handkerchief, and starts to rub his fingermarks on the pantry door.

But everywhere he goes, his filthy old galoshes make more mud-marks on the floor, and everywhere he wipes, his dirty old red handkerchief just smears the grime across and leaves everything twice as dirty as before.

'You're putting on more dirt than you're taking off!' exclaims Tom.

'I'm doing my best!' whimpers Old Man Try-By-Night, and he rubs the pantry door with his mucky sleeve, and leaves a great smear of chocolate right across it. Then he kneels down on the floor and tries to wipe up the muddy marks from his filthy old galoshes, but his knees are covered in grease and his hands are covered in chocolate and the floor gets worse and worse wherever he goes.

'Stop it! Stop it!' cries Tom. 'I'll have to clear up myself!' And he grabs a bucket and a scrubbing brush, and goes round after the old man, cleaning up and cleaning up . . . And Tom starts feeling tired and sleepy . . . but the kitchen's still covered in mud and chocolate, and the more Old Man Try-By-Night tries to clean it up, the worse it gets. Tom just can't keep up with his bucket and scrubbing brush, and just as he's beginning to think maybe he should unlock the back door and get rid of Old Man Try-By-Night once and for all, he suddenly finds it's gone dark and he can't see.

Tom's blood runs cold, for he's just realized

that Old Man Try-By-Night has crept up behind him, while he was busy scrubbing, and has tied that dirty old red handkerchief over his eyes . . .

And Old Man Try-By-Night is saying: 'This is what happens if you go prowling around the house at night, when you ought to be asleep. You never wake up in the morning!'

Tom twists from side to side, and tries to pull the dirty old red handkerchief away from his eyes, when he suddenly realizes that it's not the dirty old red handkerchief but Old Man Try-By-Night's grimy hand round his eyes! Tom manages to pull it away, but then he notices a strange thing: Old Man Try-By-Night's hand isn't grimy at all!

Then Tom looks up and he sees that it isn't even Old Man Try-By-Night! It's his father! And the morning light is streaming in through the bedroom window, and Tom is safe and sound in his own bed.

'You see? This is what happens if you go prowling round the house at night,' his father is saying. 'You never wake up in the morning!'

'But Old Man Try-By-Night . . .' says Tom. 'He's made such a mess in the kitchen!'

And Tom's father says: 'Tom, I think you've been dreaming.'

Oh yes! That's the other thing that Old Man Try-By-Night does that I can never remember. After he's woken everybody up by rattling the windows and banging the doors, he takes out his dirty old red handkerchief, and he opens it up, and there −

inside – are all manner of dreams. And before he goes, Old Man Try-By-Night chooses one or two for us, and leaves them on the doorstep – to keep us company through the night.

TOBY TICKLER

Toby had a tickle. It was a really good tickle. He could tickle anybody – even the most unticklish sort of person – and make them laugh.

Now it just so happened that His Lordship The Royal Treasurer Of The Realm was exactly that sort of person – extremely unticklish. In fact, he hadn't laughed for twenty years.

'Oh, for goodness' sake, Franklin,' the King would say to him. 'It's so gloomy having you around. Why don't you smile sometimes?'

'I smile exactly as often as is necessary,' said His Lordship The Royal Treasurer Of The Realm, and he demonstrated his smile to the King.

'If that's a smile,' said the King, 'I'm a left-handed corkscrew!'

'I beg your pardon?' said the Royal Treasurer.

'Smiling isn't like gold, you know,' said the King. 'You can't use it up or run out of it!'

'I don't care to squander anything unnecessarily, Your Majesty,' replied the Royal Treasurer, and went off to organize the day's business.

Now at the very moment that the Prime Minister was saying this to the King, Toby Tickler's mother was saying something very different to her son.

'Toby, my son,' she said. 'You are as dear to me as any son can be to his mother. If only love could make you fat, you'd be the plumpest boy in the whole kingdom. But look at you! You're just skin and bones, and I haven't enough money to feed us. I can't even pay the rent, and unless I do, we'll be thrown out of our house tomorrow morning.'

'Don't worry, Mother,' said Toby Tickler. 'I'll earn some money!'

'How are you going to do that?' replied his mother. 'You're too small and puny to work. All you can do is tickle people and make them laugh.'

'Very well,' said Toby, 'I'll make them laugh and then perhaps they'll give me a job.' And with that, he set off into town.

First he went to the Brickmaker and tickled him behind the right ear. Sure enough, the Brickmaker burst out laughing. In fact, he laughed so hard that he dropped his bricks. But when he'd stopped laughing, he turned on Toby Tickler and said: 'Look what you've done! I've broken my bricks! Get out of here!'

So then Toby went to the Bootmaker, and he tickled him behind the left ear. Well, the

Bootmaker threw down his hammer and nails and started to laugh, and he couldn't stop laughing for forty minutes. When he did stop, however, he turned on Toby Tickler and shouted: 'Look what you've done! You've made me waste forty precious minutes! I don't want any ticklers around here!'

So then Toby went to the Bellmaker, and tickled him on the back of his neck. The Bellmaker laughed and laughed so much that he cracked the bell he was casting. Whereupon he chased Toby Tickler out of his shop, even though he was still laughing as hard as ever.

Finally, Toby went to the palace kitchen, where he found the Cook cutting up the bacon. Toby thought he'd better not tickle him, so instead he said: 'Please let me work here. I have to earn some money − otherwise my mother and I will be thrown out of our house.'

But the Cook replied: 'It's a hard life, working in the King's kitchen, and you're all skin and bones. You'd never last a day!' And he went on cutting the bacon.

Well, of course, Toby looked at the eggs being boiled for the King's breakfast, and the bread being buttered, and his mouth began to water, as he began to remember that it was two days since he had last eaten anything.

He tried to leave, but he just couldn't take his eyes off all that food.

Suddenly he felt a hand on his shoulder. He looked up into the face of one of the pantrymaids.

'Dearic me!' she said. 'You're as pale as pork

and as thin as breadsticks! You'd better come in and have something to eat, before you go anywhere else, young man.'

And she sat him at the pantry table, and brought him plates of porridge and hunks of bread and a little strawberry jam.

Now, it just so happened that the Princess's favourite place in the whole palace was the pantry. She would come down every morning to spend an hour with Polly the Pantrymaid. So, of course, when she came down on this particular morning, who should she find but Toby Tickler, licking his porridge plate clean.

'You've got to earn some money somehow,' agreed the Princess, when she'd heard his story. 'Isn't there anything you're good at?'

Toby shook his head gloomily. 'There's only one thing I'm good at,' he said, 'and that just gets me into trouble.'

'What about sums?' asked the Princess. 'Perhaps my father would give you a job in the counting-house?'

So the Princess took Toby's hand, and led him to the King, who was still eating his breakfast (it used to take him most of the morning). But the King shook his head. 'You don't look serious enough for the counting-house, I'm afraid. His Lordship The Royal Treasurer Of The Realm would never approve.'

Just at that moment the Royal Treasurer came in, looking very solemn.

'Your Majesty!' he said in his gravest manner.

'Oh dear,' muttered the King. 'Here comes Cheerful Charlie.'

'There are three men at the door,' continued the Royal Treasurer, looking more and more solemn, 'who wish you to hear their complaints.'

'Oh dear, do I really have to?' sighed the King.

'It's a most serious matter!' exclaimed the Royal Treasurer.

'I thought it would be,' said the King. 'Very well, show them in.'

So the Royal Treasurer Of The Realm showed in the three men. They were the Brickmaker, the Bootmaker and the Bellmaker. As soon as they saw Toby Tickler, of course, they all three pointed at him and cried:

'That's him!'

'That's who?' asked the King.

'He made me laugh,' exclaimed the Brickmaker, 'so hard that I dropped a whole tray of new-baked bricks and broke them. I demand a good penny for the bricks I broke!'

'Well, he made me laugh so hard,' said the Bootmaker, 'that I wasted forty precious minutes. I demand a silver sixpence for the boots I could have made in that time.'

'And I demand a golden guinea!' exclaimed the Bellmaker, 'for the bell I cracked when he made me laugh.'

'Is this right?' demanded His Lordship The Royal Treasurer Of The Realm. 'You made all these people laugh?'

'It's right enough, and I'm sorry enough,' said Toby Tickler.

'Then,' said the Royal Treasurer, 'you must pay for every single thing — or I'll have you thrown into jail by your ears!'

'I can't pay anybody for anything!' cried Toby Tickler. 'My mother and I haven't even enough to pay our rent or buy our food.'

'That's your look-out!' shouted the Royal Treasurer. 'Guards! Seize this boy by the ears, and throw him in jail!'

As the guards came forward to arrest Toby Tickler, the Royal Treasurer put his face right up against Toby's and said: 'Perhaps this will teach you that there is a time and a place for everything.'

Well, I don't really know why it was, but His Lordship The Royal Treasurer Of The Realm looked so serious and so solemn that Toby Tickler just couldn't help himself . . . Just as the guards were grabbing him by the ears, he reached out his hand and tickled His Lordship under the chin.

Of course, the Royal Treasurer burst out laughing. In fact, he fell on the floor and rolled around, laughing and laughing and laughing.

'Amazing!' exclaimed the King. 'I haven't seen him laugh in twenty years! Did you just do that?'

'I'm afraid it's the only thing I can do,' sighed Toby Tickler, as the guards dragged him off by the ears.

'Then you're hired!' shouted the King after him. 'Bring that boy back here!' For, by this

97

time, the guards had already dragged Toby out of the breakfast room and halfway down the steps to the dungeon, so they promptly turned about and dragged him all the way back again – still by his ears. (It was very painful.)

Some time later, the King explained Toby's duties to him: 'There certainly is a time and place for everything – especially laughter,' he said. 'You are hereby engaged to make His Lordship The Royal Treasurer Of The Realm smile at least thirty times every day and laugh out loud at least once!'

Well, that's how Toby Tickler found a job at last, and saved his mother and himself from being thrown out of their house.

As a matter of fact, it turned out that he was good at sums after all, so when His Lordship The Royal Treasurer Of The Realm retired, Toby got his job. Although by that time he didn't really need a job any more, because he'd already married the Princess. You see . . . she sometimes liked Toby to tickle her too!

The Cat with Two Tails

In the olden days all cats had two tails – one for the daytime and one for the night. During the day they kept their long, thick daytime tail curled around themselves and slept tight and snug. But when it grew dark – ah! then each cat would go to a secret place and there it would reach in its paw and pull out a bundle wrapped in mouse-fur. Then it would wait until it was sure . . . absolutely sure . . . that nobody and nothing . . . absolutely nothing . . . was looking. (For cats, you must know, are crafty as only cats can be.) And then it would unwrap the bundle of mouse-fur, and there, inside, would be its own – its very own – night-time tail.

Its night-time tail was an ordinary length and an ordinary thickness, but it would twitch as it lay there in the bundle of mouse-fur. And although it was only an ordinary length and an ordinary thickness, it was nevertheless a very remarkable tail indeed.

Can you guess why? Well . . . I'll tell you . . . It

shone – as bright as day. And every cat would *off!* with its daytime tail in the twinkling of an eye, and *on!* with its shining night-time tail. And they'd hold their tails above their heads, and light the night as bright as day, and all the mice would tremble in the darkest corners of their holes.

When the cats stepped out, the badgers and the foxes would stop whatever they were doing to watch and clap. But every family of mice huddled together deeper in their holes, and their whiskers shook.

When the cats stepped out, the weasels and the stoats would stand on each others' shoulders to get a better view, but the mouse babies crept closer into their mothers' arms.

Now one day, a certain mouse said: 'I've had enough!'

And his wife replied: 'You're always right, of course, my dear. But enough of what? We haven't had anything to eat for days.'

'That's right!' said the mouse. 'We've had nothing to eat because those cats sleep outside our holes all day, wrapped up in their long, thick daytime tails. And at night, just when you'd think it would be safe to tiptoe out and steal a piece of cheese . . .'

'Just *one* piece of cheese!' twittered all his children.

'Those cats put on their night-time tails, and light the night as bright as day!'

'You never spoke a truer word, my dear,' said

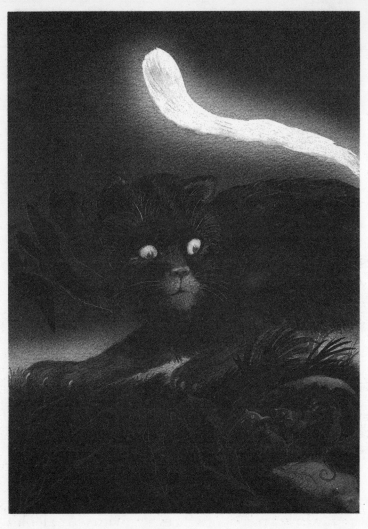

his wife. 'Those cats are crafty as only cats can be . . .'

'*That's* why I've had enough!' exclaimed the mouse, and he banged his paw on the nest. And his children felt very frightened – as they always did whenever their father got cross.

'So, since nobody else seems to be doing anything, I, Frederick Ferdinand Fury-Paws The Forty-Fourth, intend to do something about it!'

'Oh, do be careful!' twittered his wife, who was always alarmed when her husband used his full name. 'Don't do anything rash, my dear! Don't let your strength and size lead you to do things you might regret!'

But before you could say 'cheesefeathers!' that mouse had scuttled off to the Father Of All Things, and made his complaint.

The Father Of All Things listened with his head on one side. And then he listened with his head on the other side.

Then he turned to the Mother Of All Cats, who was pretending to be asleep nearby, and said: 'Well, Mother Of All Cats? It doesn't seem fair that you should have two tails when every other creature has only one.'

'Oh, I don't know,' replied the Mother Of All Cats. 'Some creatures have two legs, some creatures have four legs, some creatures have six legs and some – like the ungrateful centipede – have a hundred! So why shouldn't us cats have two tails?'

'Because,' said the mouse, 'it's unfair to us mice. You can see us by day *and* by night! We don't stand a chance.'

And so they argued all day long, until the Father Of All Things said: 'Enough! All creatures have only one head. And as it is with the head, so it should be with the tail.'

At this all the mice cheered. But the Mother Of All Cats twitched her crafty whiskers and smiled and said: 'Very true. Therefore let us cats have only one tail in future – but do you agree to let us choose which sort of tail?'

The Father Of All Things turned to the mouse and asked: 'Do you agree to this?'

And the mouse replied: 'Yes! Yes! But only the one tail!'

So the Father Of All Things said: 'Very well, you may choose.'

'Then,' said the Mother Of All Cats, giving her tail a crafty flick, 'please take note that we cats choose the sort of tail that is thick and long to keep us warm (like our daytime tails) *and* shining bright to light the night (just like our night-time tails) – both at the same time.'

'That reply was crafty as only a cat's can be,' said the Father Of All Things.

And all the other mice turned on Frederick Ferdinand Fury-Paws The Forty-Fourth and said: 'There! Now see what your meddling's done! It'll be twice as bad as it was before!'

The mouse bent his whiskers to the floor and cried out: 'Oh, please, Father Of All Things, don't allow the cats to have tails that are like their daytime tails *and* like their night-time tails both at the same time, or, I fear, we mice will all be destroyed!'

But the Father Of All Things replied: 'I cannot go back on my word.' And he turned to the

Mother Of All Cats, who was sitting sleek and crafty as only cats can be, and he said:

'Mother Of All Cats, do you promise to be satisfied if I give you a tail that is like your daytime tail and like your night-time tail – both at the same time?'

And the Mother Of All Cats smiled a crafty smile, and said: 'I agree.'

And all the cats and stoats and weasels cheered, and the baby mice crept even further into their mothers' arms and their fathers wrung their paws in despair.

'Then, from this day forth,' said the Father Of All Things, 'let all cats' tails be like their night-time tails – ordinary in size, neither thick nor long. And let them be also like their daytime tails – not shining bright to light the night – but just ordinary tails.'

And no sooner had the Father Of All Things said this, than there was a crack and a whizz, and all the cats' tails turned into ordinary tails, very much like they are today.

When they saw that, all the mice cheered, and the cats blew on their whiskers and slunk off into the forest.

But now I have to tell you a terrible thing, which goes to show that cats really are as crafty as only cats can be.

That very night – the mouse said to his wife: 'My dear, now it is dark, let us go for a promenade, for – thanks to my efforts – it is now perfectly safe to walk abroad at eventide, since cats no longer have tails that are shining bright to light the night, and they will not be able to see us.'

And his wife said: 'As always, my dear, you know best.'

And so they put on their best summer coats and frocks, and they stepped out of their hole and at once were pounced upon by the cat. For cats, of course, have all got special night-time eyes, and have always been able to see as perfectly well by night as they can by day – with or without their shining tails.

They really are as crafty as only cats can be . . .

There was once a devil in Hell named
Carnifex, who like to eat small children.
Sometimes he would take them alive and
crush all the bones in their bodies. Sometimes he
would pull their heads off, and sometimes he would
hit them so hard that their backs snapped like dry
twigs – Oh! There was no end to the terrible
things he could do. But one day, Carnifex got out
of his bed in Hell to find there was not a single
child left in his larder.

'What I need is a regular supply,' he said to
himself. So he went to a country that he knew was
ruled by an exceedingly vain king. He found him
in his bathroom (which contained over a hundred
baths) and said to him: 'How would you like to
fly?'

'Very much indeed,' said the King, 'but what
do you want in return, Carnifex?'

'Oh . . . nothing very much,' replied Carnifex,
'and I will enable you to fly as high as you want,

as fast as you want, simply by raising your arms like this,' and he showed the King how he could fly.

'I should indeed like to be able to do that,' thought the King to himself. 'But what is it you want in return, Carnifex?' he asked aloud.

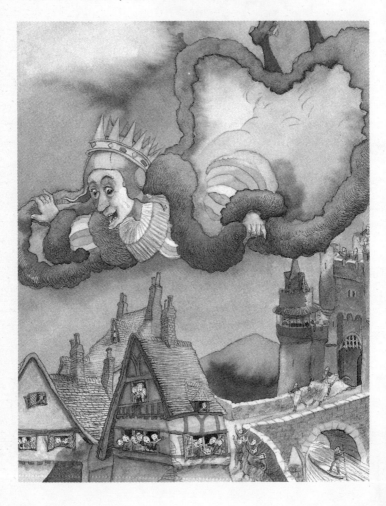

'Look! Have a try!' replied Carnifex. 'Put out your arms – that's right, and now off you go!'

The King put out his arms, and immediately floated into the air. Then he soared over the roofs and chimney-pots of the city. He went higher and higher, until he was above the clouds, and he flew like a bird on a summer's day. Then he landed back beside the devil and said:

'But what is it you want in return, Carnifex?'

'Oh, nothing very much,' replied Carnifex. 'Just give me one small child every day, and you shall be able to fly – just like that.'

Now the King was indeed very anxious to be able to fly – just like that – but he knew the terrible things that Carnifex did to small children, so he shook his head.

'But there are thousands of children in your kingdom,' replied Carnifex. 'I shall only take one a day – your people will hardly notice.'

The King thought long and hard about this, for he knew it was an evil thing, but the idea of walking anywhere, now he'd tasted the thrill of flying, seemed to him so slow and dull that in the end he agreed. And from that day on he could fly – just like that.

To begin with all his subjects were very impressed. The first time he took to the air, a great crowd gathered in the main square and stood there open-mouthed as they watched their king spread out his arms, rise into the air, and then soar up beyond the clouds and out of sight. Then he swooped down again and flew low over their heads, while they all clapped and cheered.

But after a few months it became such a common sight to see their king flying up over the city that they ceased to think anything of it. In fact some of them even began to resent it. And every day some poor family would find that one of their children had been taken by Carnifex the devil.

Now the King's youngest daughter had a favourite doll that was so lifelike that she loved it and treated it just as if it were a real live baby. And she was in the habit of stealing into the King's bathroom (when he wasn't looking) to bath this doll in one of his baths. Well it so happened that she was doing this on the very day that the King made his pact with Carnifex, and thus she overheard every word that passed between them.

Naturally she was terrified by what she had heard, but because girls were not reckoned much of in that country in those days, and because she was the least and most insignificant of all his daughters, she had not dared tell anyone what had happened. One day, however, Carnifex came and took the King's own favourite son.

The King busied himself in his counting-house, and would not say a word. Later that day he went off for a long flight, and did not return until well after dark. But the boy's mother was so overcome with grief that she took to her bed and seemed likely to die.

Then the youngest daughter came to her, as

always clutching her favourite doll, and told her all she knew.

At once the Queen's grief turned to anger against the King. But she was a shrewd woman, and she knew that if she went to the King and complained, he would – as like as not – have her head chopped off before she could utter another word. So, instead, she dressed herself as a beggar-woman, and, taking her youngest daughter with her, crept out of the palace at dead of night.

Then she went about the kingdom, far and wide, begging her way. And everywhere she went, she got her youngest daughter to stand on a stool, still clutching her favourite doll (which everyone thought was real) and tell her story. And everyone who heard the tale said: 'So that's how the King can fly!' And they were all filled with anger against the King.

Eventually all the people from all the corners of the realm came to the King to protest. They gathered in the main square, and the King hovered above them looking distinctly uneasy.

'You are not worthy to be our king!' the people cried. 'You have sacrificed our very children just so that you can fly!'

The King fluttered up a little higher, so he was just out of reach, and then he ordered them all to be quiet, and called out: 'Carnifex! Where are you?'

There was a flash and a singeing smell, and Carnifex the devil appeared, sitting on top of the fountain in the middle of the square.

At once a great cry went up from the crowd –
something between fear and anger – but Carnifex
shouted: 'Listen! I understand how you feel!'

The people were rather taken aback by these
words, and one or two of them began to think that
perhaps Carnifex wasn't such a bad fellow after
all. Some of the ladies even began to notice that
he was quite handsome – in his devilish sort of
way . . . But the King's youngest daughter stood
up on her stool, and cried out: 'He's a devil! Don't
listen to him!'

'Quite, quite,' said Carnifex, licking his lips at
the sight of the little girl still clutching her favourite doll. 'But even I can sympathize with the
tragic plight of parents who see their own beloved
offspring snatched away in front of their very eyes.'

'Well, fancy that!' said more than one citizen
to his neighbour.

'Whoever would have thought he would be
such a gentleman . . .' whispered more than one
housewife to her best friend.

'Don't listen!' shouted the King's youngest
daughter.

'So I'll tell you what I'll do,' said Carnifex,
never taking his beady eyes off the little girl clutching what he thought was a small baby. 'I'll give
you some compensation for your tragic losses. I
will let you *all* fly – just like that!' And he pointed
to the King, who flew up and down a bit and then
looped-the-loop, just to show them all what it was
like.

And there was not a single one of those good people who wasn't filled with an almost unbearable desire to join him in the air.

'Don't listen to him!' shouted the little girl. 'He'll want your children!'

'All I ask,' said Carnifex in his most wheedling voice, 'is for one tiny . . . weeny . . . little child a day. Surely that's not too much to ask?'

And, you know, perhaps there were one or two there who were so besotted with the desire to fly that they might have agreed, had not a remarkable thing happened. The King's youngest daughter suddenly stood up on tiptoe, and held up her favourite doll so that all the crowd could see, and she cried out: 'Look! This is what he'll do to your children!' And with that, she hurled the doll, which she loved so dearly, right into Carnifex's lap.

Well, of course, this was too much for the devil. He thought it was a real live baby, and he had its head off and all its limbs torn apart before you could say 'Rabbits!'

And when the crowd saw Carnifex apparently tearing a small baby to pieces (for none of them knew it was just a doll) they came to their senses at once. They gave an angry cry, and converged on Carnifex where he crouched, with his face all screwed up in disgust, spitting out bits of china and stuffing.

And I don't know what they would have done if they'd laid hold of him, but before they could, Carnifex had leapt from the fountain right on to the back of the flying king, and with a cry of rage and disappointment, he rode him down to Hell where they both belonged.

And, after that, the people gave the youngest daughter a new doll that was just as lifelike as the previous one, and she was allowed to bath it in the King's bathroom any day she wanted.

As for Carnifex, he returned every year to try and induce the people to give up just one child a day to him. But no matter what he offered them, they never forgot what they had seen him do that day, and so they refused, and he had to return empty-handed.

And all this happened hundreds and hundreds of years ago, and Carnifex never did think of anything that could persuade them.

But listen! You may think that Carnifex was a terrible devil, and you may think that the flying king was a terrible man for giving those poor children to Carnifex just so that he could fly. But I shall tell you something even more astonishing, and that is that in this very day, in this very land where you and I live, we allow not one . . . not two . . . not three . . . but twenty children to have their heads smashed or their backs broken or to be crushed alive every day – and not even so that we can fly, but just so that we can ride about in things we call motor cars.

If I'd read that in a fairy tale, I wouldn't have believed it – would you?

THE DANCING HORSE

A farmer was walking down the road one day, when he saw the most extraordinary sight. One of his horses, who should have been grazing in the field with all the other horses, was dancing.

The farmer rubbed his eyes, and then he looked again, as the horse skipped around the field on two legs, turning pirouettes and wheeling and bowing and curtsying around and around the field.

Eventually the farmer yelled to the horse: 'Hey! what do you think you're doing?'

And the horse replied: 'I hear this music in my head that makes me want to dance.'

And on it went, round and around the field.

Well, the farmer said to himself: 'People would pay a lot to see such an extraordinary sight as a dancing horse!'

So he took the horse to market, and charged

people a penny to come and see it. When everyone had assembled, the town fiddler played a jig on his fiddle, and the farmer led out his dancing horse.

But the horse just stood there and didn't dance a single step.

Well, of course, the audience booed and the farmer had to give them their money back. And when they'd gone, he turned on the horse and said: 'What's the matter? Why didn't you dance?'

'I didn't feel like it,' replied the horse. 'I couldn't hear the music in my head.'

'Didn't *feel* like it!' exclaimed the farmer. 'Listen here! You've made me a laughing-stock! I'll not feed you again – not so much as a single oat – until you dance!'

Then he took a stick and beat the horse.

Then, once again, the farmer gathered a crowd, and they each paid a penny to see the wonderful dancing horse. Once again the fiddler played a jig, but once again the horse didn't dance a single step. It was so miserable, it just stood there all the time the fiddler played.

Well, of course, the farmer was more furious than ever. He turned on the horse and shouted at it: 'Listen to me! Either you dance, or I'll sell you to the glue factory, where you'll be boiled up to make glue!'

The horse was naturally very frightened by this. And so, when the farmer once again summoned the crowd, and they'd paid their pennies, and the fiddler played his jig, the poor horse tried to dance. But its heart was so heavy that its feet were like lead, and the noise of the fiddler's jig blotted out all the sound of the music in its head.

Pretty soon the crowd started jeering again.

'Call that a dancing horse?'

'My cat dances better than that!' they yelled, and demanded their money back. The farmer turned on the horse, white with anger, for he'd never touched so much money before, and now he was having to give it all back.

'You lazy, ungrateful creature!' he shouted at the horse. And there and then he took it and sold it to the glue factory.

Now it so happened that the day was Sunday and the glue factory was not working until the next morning. So the horse was put into a field to wait.

When it found itself back in a field of grass, it was so happy to be away from all those staring faces and its cruel owner, that it started to hear the music in its head once more. And once again it started to dance around the field – a sad but graceful dance.

And there, I believe, it is still dancing to this day, for the owner of the glue factory happened to look out of his window and saw the horse dancing so beautifully in the field below. And he said to himself: 'Clearly this is a mare that dances for love not money.'

And he let her dance in that field as long as she lived and heard the music in her head.

MACK AND MICK

Once upon a time were two brothers who could never agree about anything. They argued about what to have for breakfast. They argued about what to have for lunch. They even argued about which side of the bed they should sleep on.

One day Mack said to Mick: 'I can't stand living with you another day. I'm leaving!'

'No you're not!' exclaimed Mick. 'I can't stand living with *you* another day. *I'm* the one that's leaving!'

Well, they argued and they argued and they argued about which one of them was to leave, but they just couldn't agree. So, in the end, they both left.

They marched along the road that led to the great wide world, and when they reached the crossroads, Mick turned to Mack and said: 'Goodbye, Mack. I'm taking this road that leads to the sea.'

'No you're not!' shouted Mack. 'That's my road! You'll have to take the road to the hills.'

Well, they stood there arguing for about an hour, but they couldn't agree about which road the other was taking. So in the end, they both set off along the same road. And pretty soon they came to the sea.

'Ah!' said Mick. 'I can't wait to put an ocean between us two.'

'Neither can I,' said Mack.

When they got to the harbour, however, they found there was only one ship due to sail.

Could they agree which of them was to take it? No, of course they couldn't. 'I was the first to say I wanted to put an ocean between us,' said Mick.

'But I was the first to say I wanted to leave!' exclaimed Mack. So they stood on the quay, and they argued and they argued and they argued – until they saw the ship weighing its anchor, and they both had to leap aboard – otherwise they'd both have missed it.

As soon as they got on board they started arguing again, and they didn't stop once.

Their crewmates quickly grew tired of them.

'Don't you two ever agree about anything?' the other sailors asked.

'No,' said Mack and Mick together. 'Never!' And they carried on arguing about which of them felt the more seasick.

Eventually the Captain could stand it no longer, and he made them sleep down in the hold of the ship, away from the rest of the crew.

But, even down in the hold, the entire ship's company could still hear Mack and Mick arguing and arguing and arguing as bad as ever.

So the Captain hauled them up on deck in front of the whole crew, and said: 'We are all sick and tired of your constant bickering. It sets our teeth on edge all day, and it keeps us awake all night. So here's what I'm going to do. Either you two stop arguing, or I'm going to throw you off the ship at the next desert island we come to.'

Mack immediately turned to Mick. 'See?' he said. 'This is all your fault.'

'What are you talking about?' exclaimed Mick. 'I wouldn't be arguing if it weren't for you! It's all *your* fault.'

And they were taken down into the hold again still arguing and arguing.

Well, the ship sailed on for seven days and seven nights, until one morning the look-out shouted: 'Land ahead!'

The Captain looked through his telescope and saw a desert island on the horizon. Once again he summoned Mack and Mick up on to the deck in front of the whole crew and he said: 'I'll give you one last chance. If you can keep yourselves from arguing as long as that desert island is in sight, you can stay on board. But if you have so much as one argument, I'll throw you overboard, and you'll have to live out the rest of your lives on that island.'

Well, Mack looked at Mick, and Mick looked at Mack. Then Mack said: 'Well, Mick, if anyone starts an argument – it'll be you.'

'That's a laugh, Mack!' exclaimed Mick. 'You're much more likely to start an argument than I am!'

And with that, of course, they started arguing again, and they didn't stop until the ship reached the desert island, and the two of them were thrown overboard and they had to swim for the shore.

Mack and Mick stood on the shore of the desert island, and watched their ship disappear over the horizon.

'Well this is a pretty how's yer father!' said Mack. 'We try to get away from each other . . .'

'And we end up marooned together on a desert island,' said Mick.

'Exactly,' said Mack.

There wasn't much to eat on that desert island. For breakfast they managed to find two clams, so they ate one each. For lunch they managed to catch a dodo (I'm afraid it was the last one).

Normally they would have argued about whether to roast or boil it, but as they didn't have any pots or pans they had no choice. They stuck it on a stick, and held it over the fire. And it tasted pretty good.

As night began to fall, they broke branches off a tree and made themselves a rough shelter by the beach. There they sat together, looking out into the night sea, hoping their ship would return to pick them up. But it didn't. And they fell asleep, trying to remember the names of the flowers that grew in their garden back home.

The next day, they searched the island and found a sparkling stream of fresh water. There they decided to build a house. Then they lit a fire at the top of the nearby hill to attract the attention of any ship that might pass by.

'We must make sure we keep it burning . . .' said Mick.

'Day and night,' said Mack.

But that night, as they sat down to a meal of fresh fish, they heard the wind begin to blow.

'Looks like there's going to be a storm,' said Mick.

'You're right,' said Mack. 'We'd better tie the roof on.'

So they tied the roof down with creepers from the forest, as the wind blew stronger and fiercer. Then the rain began to lash the island. Before long, Mick and Mack were cowering in their log house, listening to the thunder breaking over their heads, and watching bolts of lightning striking out of the sky.

Suddenly there was a terrible noise and the sound of breaking branches.

'Run!' cried Mick.

'I am!' cried Mack.

And they ran as hard as they could out into the storm, just as a huge tree came crashing down on their log house, smashing it to pieces.

Still the wind blew even fiercer, and the rain lashed across their backs, and the water ran down their faces like sheets of tears.

'We must find shelter!' said Mick.

'Over there!' cried Mack. And they started running towards a cave. They reached the cave just as the wind began to turn into a hurricane. It blew away the remnants of their house as if it had been matchwood.

The lightning hit tree after tree, and fire swept across the island. Mack and Mick trembled, holding on to each other in the safety of the cave.

As day broke, the storm subsided, but as it did, their troubles redoubled. They awoke to a roar that made their blood run cold.

Mack and Mick both sat bolt upright, and stared in horror, for there in the mouth of the cave was a huge monster with a head as big as its own body. When it opened its jaws and roared again, both Mack and Mick thought they were going to tumble into it − its throat seemed so vast and deep.

The monster advanced into the cave, and looked from Mack to Mick and from Mick to Mack.

Mack backed away towards one side of the cave, and Mick backed towards the other, as the terrible creature took another step further into the cave. First it turned towards Mick and showed its razor-sharp teeth. Then it turned towards Mack and stretched out a razor-sharp claw.

'It can't make up its mind *which* of us looks tastiest!' cried Mick.

'Well let's not give it the chance to find out!' shouted Mack.

'Ready?' shouted Mick.

'Ready!' screamed Mack. And they both together sprinted for the entrance of the cave as fast as fear could take them. First the monster darted towards Mick, then it turned towards Mack, but by then Mack was out of the cave, and so was Mick!

'See you on the other side of the island!' shouted Mick.

'Right!' yelled Mack. And they both ran off in opposite directions, and the monster stood roaring in the cave mouth, hopping from one foot to the other, unable to decide whether to chase after Mick or chase after Mack.

So it was that Mack and Mick found themselves on separate sides of the island.

Mack found himself amongst quicksands and deep dark bogs that nearly sucked him down on several occasions . . . until he had the idea of tying branches to his feet so that he didn't sink in.

Mick found himself in a dark forest, infested with wild wolves. He armed himself as best he could with a stout stick and a knife, and pursued his way. But he could hear the wolves following him, and he could see their eyes glinting in the blackness of the forest.

Mick wished he had Mack with him to give him courage. And Mack wished he had Mick with him to help him every time he fell into a bog.

At length, however, they met up together on the other side of the island.

'Thank goodness!' cried Mick.

'It's good to see you!' cried Mack.

But no sooner had they hugged each other and done a little dance of joy, than an even worse calamity befell them!

They heard a terrible explosion above, and they looked up – in time to see the top blow off the volcano in the centre of the island and flames begin to shoot up into the sky. A great cloud of soot shot up into the air and covered the sun. The next minute, they saw molten rock bubbling up over the rim of the crater and down the sides of the mountain towards them.

'The sea!' cried Mack.

'Here we go again!' yelled Mick, and they both plunged into the sea, and started to swim . . . But even as they hit the water, the white-hot molten lava flowed over the shore.

And they had swum no further than the shadow of the mountain at mid-morn, when the lava reached the sea. The air was filled with an ear-splitting hiss, and the island disappeared in a cloud of steam, as the water started to bubble.

'Help!' yelled Mick. 'The sea's boiling!'

'We'll be cooked – like the ogre in the next story!' cried Mack. And they both swam as hard as they could, until – as fate would have it – they reached cooler water. But the smiles on their faces quickly disappeared as they looked around them:

'Sharks!' screamed Mick.

'I don't believe it!' screamed Mack. But sure enough, they could see sharks circling all around them.

'Look out!' screamed Mack. 'Here comes one!'

'What a way to go!' yelled Mack. 'After all we've been through!'

But, just at very that moment, white-hot ash

started to fall out of the sky.

'Dive!' yelled Mick. And the two brothers dived, while the hot ash fell on the sharks, and the sharks were so confused they thrashed the sea, and then turned on their tails and swam off.

Some time later, Mack and Mick found themselves clinging to a tree trunk, on which they drifted for two days and two nights. On the third day, however, the breeze blew them on to a little sandy island with two trees in the middle of it.

They lay there gasping, and wondered what else could possibly happen to them, until they both fell asleep from exhaustion, and didn't wake up until the next day.

When they opened their eyes they blinked and looked again, but – sure enough – they could see something on the horizon.

'It's a sail!' exclaimed Mick.

'We're saved!' exclaimed Mack. And the two of them jumped around the little island for joy.

But as the sail got closer, they began to realize it was a very strange sail indeed. In the first place it was big – bigger than any sail either of them had ever seen. The second strange thing about it was that it appeared to be made out of fish-skins, for one side was plain and the other was covered in silver scales. But – without a shadow of doubt – the very strangest thing about the sail was the fact that there was no ship under it. It was simply a giant sail of fish-skins, flying across the water.

And when it reached the island, something even stranger happened. It blew over the heads of Mack and Mick, until it reached half-way across the little island, and there the two trees caught it in their palms – as if they'd been hands – and held it tight.

The sail of fish-skins billowed out as the wind filled it once more, and then the strangest thing of all happened . . . The island itself began to move . . . It started to glide across the water like a ship – blown by the wind caught in its fish-skin sail.

Mack and Mick were so surprised and so terrified all at the same time that they held on to each other tight.

Well, the wind blew the sail, and the island sped through the seas until finally they saw ahead of them the shoreline of their own country. As they approached, the wind died down, and the little island started to sink beneath the waves, so Mack and Mick both had to swim for it, until they arrived back at the harbour from which they had first set out.

Mack and Mick crawled ashore, and as they did so they heard a voice. There, standing on a rock, was the Captain of the ship in which they'd first sailed.

'Well?' he said. 'What happened to you?'

Mack and Mick looked at each other and said: 'We've been *bored stiff*!'

And they told the Captain their adventures.

'What!' exclaimed the Captain, when they'd finished. 'Your house was destroyed by a typhoon! You were attacked by a monster! Beset by quicksands and wild beasts! You were caught under an erupting volcano! Attacked by sharks! And brought home by a magic sail! How can you possibly call that "boring"?'

'Tell him,' said Mack.

'No, you tell him,' said Mick.

'Well,' they both said together, 'we were so hard put to it that we didn't have time for a single argument!'

'But that's marvellous!' exclaimed the Captain.

'No it isn't!' replied Mack and Mick. 'Because the one thing we learnt is that we *like* arguing!'

And with that, the two brothers took their leave of the Captain, and made their way back home.

There they continued arguing to their hearts' content.

After all, the world would be a very dull place indeed if we all agreed about absolutely everything, wouldn't it?

THE SLOW OGRE

There was once an ogre who loved to eat ... CABBAGES! And he loved to eat ... SAUSAGES! And he loved to eat ... RADISHES! But best of all ... absolutely best of all ... he loved to eat ... PEOPLE!

But there's nothing so extraordinary about that, because that's what ogres do. None the less, he was a very extraordinary ogre – and I shall tell you why. He was very ... very ... very ... incredibly ... unbelievably ... wonderfully SLOW!

When he got up in the morning, it took him eight hours to get out of bed. It would take him nine hours to walk downstairs, and then it would take him ten hours to boil his breakfast of human heads and gentlemen's socks. Then it would take him fifteen hours to eat it. It would take him twenty hours to get up from the table, burp, and put on his Ogres' Boots (which are, by the way, very expensive). And it would take him another twenty-three hours to walk to his front door.

Now, as I expect you know, there are only twenty-four hours in a day, so it had already taken him three days, and all he'd done was get up and have breakfast.

He was, as you can see, a very slow ogre indeed.

Being so slow was a slight problem when it came to stealing . . . CABBAGES! out of people's gardens.

And being so slow was a slight problem when it came to snitching . . . SAUSAGES! out of butchers' shops. And being so slow made it quite difficult when it came to rustling . . . RADISHES! out of people's salad bowls. But you may well wonder how on earth . . .   how on *earth* . . . such a slow ogre could . . . even in a thousand years . . . ever manage to catch *people* to put in his breakfast stew.

Well, here's this Ogre getting up this morning. It's already taken him six days to put his coat on and leave his lair. It's taken him three weeks to walk down the road, and he's just arrived at the house of a very rich gentleman.

It's taken him half a day to knock at the gates. In the meantime nobody has come in or gone out, because . . . well you wouldn't, would you, if you had an ogre as tall as three men standing outside your gates?

But now the Gatekeeper shouts through the letterbox: 'Go away! We don't want any ogres around here, thank you very much.'

'Oh! I'm not an ogre,' says the Ogre. 'I'm just a poor fellow who has grown too big through eating ... CABBAGES! and eating ... SAUSAGES! and eating ... RADISHES! and ...'

'And?' asks the Gatekeeper.

'And nothing else,' replies the Ogre.

'I don't believe you,' cries the Gatekeeper.

'But look at me,' says the Ogre. 'I'm so slow, how could I possibly be an ogre?'

So the Gatekeeper looks out of the window, and he sees the Ogre moving so slowly . . . so extraordinarily slowly . . . that he barely seems to be moving at all.

'Anybody could run away from me before I'd got the chance to grab 'em and rip off their heads and boil 'em up for a delicious breakfast stew . . . I mean a disgusting breakfast stew,' says the Ogre.

'That's true,' says the Gatekeeper. 'Maybe I'll open the gate.'

But the Gatekeeper's Daughter says: '*Daddy! Don't let him in!*'

So the Gatekeeper shouts back to the Ogre: 'But before I open the gate, first tell me what you want.'

And the Ogre replies: 'Oh! I just want to do an honest day's work, in return for a dinner of . . . CABBAGES! and . . . SAUSAGES! and . . . RADISHES! and . . .'

'And?' says the Gatekeeper.

'And absolutely nothing else at all,' replies the Ogre.

'Honestly?' asks the Gatekeeper.

'Honestly,' replies the Ogre.

'Well, in that case, maybe I'll open the gate,' says the Gatekeeper. 'We could use someone as big as you to put up the Christmas holly.'

But the Gatekeeper's Daughter cries: '*Daddy!*

Don't let him in!'

'I'll tell you what,' says the Ogre. 'I'll put up the Christmas holly and I'll put on a show for all the little kiddies.'

'Well that would be very nice,' says the Gatekeeper, 'but maybe I should just check with the Master of the House.'

So he goes to the Master of the House, and the Master of the House says: 'He sounds like an ogre to me.'

'But he says he'll put up the holly and put on a nice Christmas show for the children,' says the Gatekeeper.

'Oh! That would be very nice,' says the Master of the House. 'Maybe we should let him in after all.'

But the Gatekeeper's Daughter yells: 'Looks like an ogre – *is* an ogre! *Daddy! Don't let him in!'*

'What's she doing here?' cries the Master of the House. 'I don't want to be told what I can and can't do in my own house!' And he has the Gatekeeper's Daughter trussed up like a turkey and locked in the Tall Tower.

Then he and the Gatekeeper go to the gate and look through the letterbox.

'Hmm,' says the Master of the House. 'He may put on a very nice show for the children, but he's as tall as three men and he's got razor-sharp ogre's teeth. Maybe we shouldn't let him in after all.'

'Oh,' says the Ogre. 'I'm only big because I eat ... CABBAGES! and ... SAUSAGES! and ... RADISHES! and . . .'

'And?' says the Master of the House.

'Absolutely nothing else at all,' says the Gatekeeper.

'That's right,' says the Ogre. 'And my teeth are only razor-sharp because I like whistling!' And he whistles a little tune.

'Well, in that case, maybe we'll let you in,' says the Master of the House.

But the Gatekeeper's Daughter shouts down from the window in the Tall Tower: '*Daddy! Don't let him in!*'

Meanwhile the Mistress of the House has come out to see what all the shouting's about. She looks out through the letterbox and says:

'Well, he may put on a very nice show for the children, and he may put up the holly very tastefully, but he still looks like an ogre to me.'

'But he's so slow,' says the Master of the House.

'He'd never be able to catch any of us,' says the Gatekeeper.

'That's right,' says the Ogre.

'Well, in that case,' says the Mistress of the House, 'maybe he can come in.'

And, from right up in the Tall Tower, comes the voice of the Gatekeeper's Daughter: '*DADDY! DON'T LET HIM IN!*'

But the Gatekeeper has already drawn back the first bolt on the gate. And, because she's up in the Tall Tower, the Gatekeeper's Daughter can see the Ogre, on the other side of the gate, starting to lick his chops. So she yells down: 'He's going to boil your heads for his breakfast stew!'

'Fiddle-de-dee!' says the Ogre.

'Fiddle-de-dee!' says the Master of the House.

'Fiddle-de-dee!' says the Mistress of the House.

And the Gatekeeper draws back the second bolt.

Now the Gatekeeper's Daughter can see the Ogre starting to drool and slobber at the mouth.

'He's going to catch you all and pull off your heads!' she cries.

'Oh! Somebody shut her up!' says the Mistress of the House. 'Even if he were an ogre – he'd never be able to catch any of us.'

'That's right,' says the Ogre, licking his lips.

'That's right,' says the Gatekeeper. 'I'm looking forward to the Christmas show.' And he pulls back the third bolt.

Now all that separates them from the Slow Ogre is one small latch. And the Gatekeeper's Daughter can't shout out anything, because someone's tied a neckerchief round her mouth. But she's thinking: '*Daddy! Don't let him in!*'

And the Ogre's drooling and slobbering and licking his lips, and the Gatekeeper's just about to lift the latch, when he stops and says: 'Wait a minute! My daughter's a very smart girl. She's usually right about most things.'

'But she's only a child,' says the Master of the House.

'And she's still got her hair in braids,' says the Mistress of the House.

'That's true,' says the Gatekeeper, and he lifts the latch, and the Ogre bursts in and grabs everybody in the house – except for the Gatekeeper's

Daughter, because she's locked up in the Tall Tower. Then he stuffs them all into the big black bag that he always carries, and races off back to his lair — for you must know that the Slow Ogre can move *surprisingly* quickly when it's a question of making his breakfast stew.

Now, the Gatekeeper's Daughter is still trussed up like a turkey, but she manages to wriggle free. She rips the neckerchief from her mouth. Then she takes the rope with which she'd been tied, hangs it out of the window and slides down it . . . right to the ground.

Then she runs back into her father's bedroom, stuffs all his smelliest old socks into a pillowcase, and races off to the Ogre's lair.

The Ogre's got a cauldron of water coming up to the boil, and he's got all the people locked up in his great iron meat-safe. And they're all moaning and crying and blaming each other for not having taken more notice of the Gatekeeper's Daughter.

The Gatekeeper's Daughter, meanwhile, has marched straight up to the Ogre's front door and knocked on it. (That's a very brave thing to do, and I don't think even she would have done it if she hadn't had a very good plan.)

The Ogre's just thinking: 'Hm! The water's coming to the boil, so I can pop in a few heads . . . but first I need a bit of seasoning. I'd better borrow some of the gentlemen's socks . . .' (I hope you haven't forgotten that he always liked gentlemen's socks in his breakfast stew – the smellier the better.)

So he's just about to open the meat-safe and grab all the gentlemen to see who's got the smelliest socks, when he hears the knock on the door.

'S'funny!' says the Ogre to himself, 'Nobody likes me. Nobody ever comes to visit me. Nobody ever knocks on my door.'

But he goes to the door anyway (only it takes him an hour or so because he's starting to get a bit slower again) and he opens it.

There's the Gatekeeper's Daughter, holding the pillowcase full of her father's smelliest socks.

'Something smells good!' exclaims the Ogre. And he's just going to grab the Gatekeeper's Daughter to pop her into his mouth as a pre-breakfast snack, when she opens up the pillowcase, and the Ogre can't help sticking his head inside, because the Gatekeeper's socks smell so good.

Then, quick as a flash, she ties the pillowcase around his neck with the rope. And the Ogre starts flailing around, going: 'Oh! I can't see! It's all gone dark! Oh! But it's so delicious! The smell is like ... it's like ... heaven ... yum, yum, yum ...'

And while he's blundering around, getting slower and slower, unable to decide whether to take the pillowcase off his head, so he can see, or to keep it on his head, so he can go on smelling the socks, the Gatekeeper's Daughter – quick as a flash – opens up the Ogre's meat-safe and lets everyone out. They all dash for the door and run off as far away as possible from the Ogre's lair.

The Ogre, meanwhile, has decided to sit down in his favourite cosy chair, while he takes the pillowcase off his head – only he's moving *much* slower by this time. The Gatekeeper's Daughter sees what he's going to do, and – in the time it takes him to get over to his favourite cosy chair and start to sit down – she's switched it, so that instead of sitting down in his favourite cosy chair, the Ogre sits down right in the cauldron of boiling water!

By the time the Ogre's realized what's happened, and before he can get the pillowcase off his

head and get himself out again . . . he's cooked –
right through! And so are the socks!

When the Gatekeeper's Daughter gets home, her
father makes a great fuss of her and says: 'In
future, Chloë, we'll always listen to you.' And the
Master of the House and the Mistress of the House
all nod in agreement. And Chloë looks at them all
smiling down at her and she says to herself: 'Hmm!
I wonder if you will?'

THE FAST ROAD

There used to be one road that got you to wherever you wanted to go much quicker than any other road. It looked like a perfectly ordinary road. But the moment you stepped on to it, you got wherever it was you wanted to go to ... That is if you knew where you wanted to go. Unfortunately most folk weren't absolutely sure. They liked the idea of getting somewhere so much that they often stepped on to the road before they'd decided where it was that they wanted to end up.

And – when you did that – this is what would happen:

You'd step on the road and start walking. For a moment it would seem just like walking along any old road, but then, as you walked on a bit further, you'd find the countryside slipping past as though you were running – even though you were still just walking. The next minute, the countryside would be speeding past – as if you were galloping on a horse, and before you knew where you were, there would be just a blur on either side of you, as the world flashed past quicker than the eye could see . . .

And if you didn't know where you were going, it would just go on getting faster and faster until . . . all of a sudden! it would stop.

And when you looked around you, you would see this:

Nothing.

Nothing to your left. Nothing to your right. Nothing in front of you. Nothing behind you. Nothing . . . Nothing, that is, except for people wandering around quite lost.

Well, here is the story of a girl, named Poppy, who stepped on to the Fast Road, and who didn't have the first clue where she was heading.

The moment she stepped on to the Fast Road, she had an idea that something was going to happen, but she couldn't imagine what.

To begin with, of course, it was just like walking along any other road, but very soon she noticed the countryside slipping past faster than she was walking. Then, before she could work out what was happening, she found the countryside whizzing past her – as if she were galloping on a horse! And the next minute, it was all a blur – flashing past her on both sides – so fast that she couldn't make out anything. The fields were just a blur of green. Cows and sheep were like stripes of brown and white. It all went faster and faster and faster until . . . all of sudden! . . . it stopped.

Poppy almost fell over herself, it was so sudden. But she shook her head, and looked around. And do you know what she could see? That's right . . .

Nothing.

Nothing to her left. Nothing to her right. Nothing in front of her. Nothing behind her. There were plenty of people wandering around, but she could see they were quite lost.

Poppy picked herself up and said: 'Well, I wonder where I am?' Then she stepped off the road and walked across the flat nothingness towards the horizon.

After a while, she saw something in the distance, and as she got nearer, she saw that it was a strange building. It was as tall as a mountain and it was full of people. But the really extraordinary thing was that the building didn't have an inside! It was all outside!

At the bottom, was a man behind a desk.

'Can you tell me where I am?' asked Poppy.

'This is Nowhere In Particular,' replied the man. 'Would you like to sign the Guest Book?'

'I'll not sign the book,' said Poppy, 'because I'm not stopping, but is it all right if I look around?'

'Help yourself,' said the man. 'There's nothing particular here.'

So Poppy climbed the stairs that led all round the outside of the building.

On the first floor, she met a family who were sitting on stools looking at a stone.

'What on earth are you doing?' asked Poppy.

'We're stone-watching,' replied the whole family, without taking their eyes off the stone.

'Stone-watching?' said Poppy. 'I've never heard of such a thing. Isn't it extremely boring?'

'Oh no!' exclaimed the father.

'But stones don't *do* anything,' said Poppy.

'But this one *might*!' exclaimed the mother.

'And we'll be the first to see it when it does!' exclaimed the children. 'Why don't you come and join us?'

But Poppy shook her head. 'I may not know where I'm going,' she said, 'but you'll not catch me watching stones!'

And on she climbed, up the staircase that wound around the outside of the strange building.

A little further up, she found a man with a broom, sweeping the floor as hard as he could.

'Excuse me,' said Poppy, 'can you tell me where I'm going?'

'I'll tell you just as soon as I've finished getting this room clean,' he said, without once raising his head.

'But it's already as clean as clean can be!' exclaimed Poppy.

'Oh no!' said the man with the broom. 'Look! There's another speck of dust there!'

'Well,' said Poppy, 'I can't wait around for you to finish making a clean room clean.'

'But look!' exclaimed the man. 'If you took that other broom, we'd get it done in half the time!'

'Sorry,' said Poppy. 'Half of never is still never!'

And with that she climbed on her way, up the

staircase that led around the outside of the strange house.

Well, up she went, up and up, until finally she reached a place that was full of people lying on their backs with their mouths wide open.

'Excuse me!' said Poppy. 'I'm trying to find out where I'm going. Can you help me?'

But the people just lay on their backs, and they didn't close their mouths for a minute. But one of them said: ''Ooee 'ank 'elk 'oo. 'Orry.'

''Ooee 'ank 'elk 'oo?' said Poppy. 'Oh! You mean "We can't help you"!'

''At's 'ight,' said the man.

'Well, just tell me what you're doing, and then I'll get on my way,' said Poppy.

''Ooee're 'atching grocks og 'ain 'orter,' said the man.

''Ain 'orter?' said Poppy. 'Oh! Rain water! But it's not raining.'

''Ick 'ill 'oon,' said the man.

'Not today,' said Poppy.

'It's 'udderly 'orter!' said the man.

'I'm sure it's lovely water,' replied Poppy, 'but I'm on my way.'

Well, she didn't need to climb much further, before she suddenly found herself right on the top of the strange building. And from there she could see for miles and miles around. And right in the very far distance, she could see a little house, where a woman was working in the kitchen.

'Wait a minute! That's where I'm going!' she exclaimed.

And she ran down that building as fast as she possibly could, past the Mouths-Wide-Open, past the Man with the Broom, past the Stone-Watchers, and past the Man at the Gate. Then she ran and she didn't stop until she'd reached the Fast Road.

'I'm going home!' she shouted, and she started to walk. And before she'd taken a couple of steps . . . there she was – home!

'Well,' said Poppy, as she helped her mother prepare supper, 'at least I know where I'm going in future – I'm only going where I can do something useful! And I'll tell you another thing . . . I also know where I'm not going! And – what's more – I'm never taking the Fast Road to either place!'

The Song That Brought Happiness

A wandering minstrel once composed a magical song that made everyone who heard it glad. No matter how many cares weighed them down, this song made them forget them. No matter how miserable their lives, all those who listened to this song felt happy again. But the happiness, of course, only lasted as long as the song. As soon as the song ceased, everyone's cares returned.

The minstrel wandered around from country to country, singing his magical song, and bringing happiness to people for as long as he sang it. One day, however, he sang it at the court of an evil old king, who made all his subjects as miserable as he was himself. Well, the moment the minstrel began to sing his magical song, it was as if a shadow had been lifted from the entire court. Everyone forgot the injustices and humiliations that were daily

heaped upon them by the evil old King, and felt a happiness that they had forgotten existed. Even the old King himself started to smile at those around him, and for the first time in years he felt peace in his shrivelled old heart.

As soon as the song stopped, however, the deepest gloom returned to the palace.

The minstrel bowed and began to take his leave of the company, but the evil old king stopped him.

'Play that song again!' commanded the King.

'Excuse me, Your Majesty,' replied the minstrel. 'Nothing would give me greater pleasure, but I have a rule that I only play my songs once – lest I outstay my welcome.'

'I order you to play that song again,' said the King. 'Otherwise I will have you thrown into prison.'

So there was nothing for it – the minstrel had to play the song once more, and once more the gloom lifted from the palace, and everyone felt happy.

When he had finished, the minstrel once again began to take his leave, but again the old King stopped him.

'Keep singing!' he ordered. 'I will tell you when you may stop.'

So the poor minstrel was forced to go on singing the magical song that made everyone happy, over and over again, until everyone started to grow sleepy. Heads nodded and fell on to the tables, and finally the old King himself fell asleep over his plate.

Then the minstrel tried to leave once more, but

the guards barred his way.

'The King has not said you can stop singing yet,' they said, and they showed him the sharp blades of their swords.

So, once again, the minstrel had to sing the magical song, over and over again, and carry on – even though weary himself – until everyone in the palace had fallen asleep. Then he tried to steal out of the great hall.

But, as luck would have it, just as he was closing the door behind him, the old King awoke.

'Come back!' roared the King. 'I never want to feel miserable again! You must carry on playing that magical song for me, day and night!' And he appointed guards to stand by the minstrel to see that he did.

And so the wandering minstrel was compelled to remain in the palace, continually singing his magical song that made everyone feel happy.

But the minstrel did not feel happy himself. 'I cannot carry on singing this song over and over again,' he said to himself. 'I must stop to eat . . . besides, my voice will grow hoarse.'

But day and night the guards stood over him, and he had no choice but to go on singing.

Well, this went on for three days and three nights. On the fourth day, a string on his harp broke.

'I cannot play the song any more,' the minstrel said to the King. 'I don't have all the notes.'

'Carry on!' ordered the King.

*

On the fifth day, the minstrel's voice went hoarse, so that he could only croak, and all the magic went from the song.

'Your Majesty!' gasped the poor minstrel. 'Now surely you will let me stop.'

'Play on!' growled the King.

So the poor minstrel had to play on – even though he could no longer play the right notes nor sing the song, and everyone grew heartily sick of the dreadful noise he was making. Yet still the King would by no means allow him to stop.

In the end, the minstrel could stand it no longer. He flung his harp at the King's head, and it struck him right on the temple, so that he fell down dead. As soon as he did, of course, the guards drew their swords and cut down the unfortunate minstrel, and the magical song was lost for ever.

So it was that the song that brought happiness ended up bringing misery – all through one man's greed.

Touch the Moon

A long, long, time ago, a king once decided to build a tower. 'I shall build this Tower so high,' he said, 'that from its topmost battlements – if you stand on tiptoe – you will be able to touch the moon.'

'I fear,' said his Chief Architect, 'that there will not be enough stone in the whole country to build a tower so high.'

'Nonsense!' said the King. 'Get building.'

'I am afraid,' said his Chancellor, 'that there won't be enough gold in the Treasury to pay for such a building.'

'Nonsense!' said the King. 'Get taxing.'

'What is the point of being able to touch the moon?' asked his daughter.

But the King didn't hear her – he was far too busy organizing the laying of the foundations, the raising of the finances and the knocking-down of half his capital city to make way for the Tower.

The city itself was divided in two about the building of the Tower. Half the citizens thought it was a wonderful project. 'It is vital,' they said, 'that we are able to touch the moon before any of our rivals can.'

But the other half of the city (who were losing their homes and shops to make way for the Tower) were, naturally, much less enthusiastic. But even they were not against building the Tower altogether – they were just against building it in their half of the city.

'It will indeed be marvellous when we can touch the moon – just by standing on tiptoe,' they said. 'But it would make much more sense to build it on the other side of the city – the ground's higher there for a start!'

'But what is the point of touching the moon at all?' asked the King's Daughter again. But she might as well have been talking to a lump of wood. As a matter of fact, she was talking to a lump of wood! You see, the Princess had a secret . . . but I can't tell you what it was. Not just yet.

Well, they knocked down half the city, and, in its place, they started to build the gigantic Tower. The citizens who'd lost their homes had to camp outside the city wall, and they suffered in the cold winter. But no one was allowed to rebuild their house, because all the stone was needed for the Tower.

All the stone quarries in the land were ordered to send every stone they produced to help build the Tower. And the King's builders worked day and night – all through that winter and all through that summer, and, by the time winter came again, they'd built the first storey.

'The work must go faster than this!' exclaimed the King. 'Or we'll never be able to touch the moon – not even by standing on tiptoe!'

So the King gave orders that the work had to go twice as fast. No one was to take lunch breaks or tea breaks, and the mules pulling the carts had to walk twice as quickly.

And on they built – all through that winter. Soon the quarries ran out of stone, and they began digging new quarries in fields where animals used to graze.

And on they built, until by the end of that year, they'd finished the second storey.

'Loafers! Do-nothings! Time-wasters! Afternoon farmers!' exclaimed the King. 'We'll never be able to touch the moon at this rate!'

Then he gave orders that half of his subjects must give up their usual jobs, and work instead upon the Tower. And on the building went.

The countryside began to disappear as quarries took the place of farms. Food became scarce, and everybody in the land suffered.

'This is CRAZY!' shouted the King's Daughter. 'My dad's gone loony! He's ruining his own kingdom, and for what? Just so some idiots can stand on tiptoe and touch the moon!'

But the lumps of wood she was talking to didn't reply. They just lay there, the way that lumps of wood do.

'You've got more sense than my dad!' she exclaimed. 'And you're just two short planks!'

Meanwhile the building went on and on. The citizens suffered more and more each day, but they kept telling each other that it would be all worth it, once they could touch the moon.

Eventually they completed the third storey. But the King's coffers were now empty, there was scarcely any food, and life was miserable.

By the time the fourth storey had been completed, most of the kingdom had been carried away in carts as stone for the building. The green fields had disappeared, the woods and forests had all been chopped down, and all that was left was the Tower.

And now even the citizens themselves began to complain. They sent some representatives to the King, who fell on their knees in front of him, and said:

'O King! Of course we all know the vital importance to our country of being able to touch the moon, but we have hardly anything left to eat, the kingdom has been turned into one vast quarry, and life has become intolerable. Please may we stop?'

But the King just became furious, and he ordered his army to compel every single person in the kingdom to work on the Tower.

And so they built the fifth storey.

It was at this moment that the King's Daughter,

who was, by this time, a fine young girl of sixteen, said:

'I am going to put a stop to this nonsense once and for all.'

And now the time has come when I must tell you the Princess's secret. Only you mustn't tell anyone else because . . . well . . . she liked doing something that Princesses aren't really supposed to like doing. In fact, it was something which she only did if she was sure – absolutely sure – that nobody else, except her most trusted chambermaid, was around. I wonder if you can guess what it was? Well . . . I suppose I'd better tell you . . . The Princess was very keen . . . very keen indeed . . . on carpentry!

Now in those days, the only people who normally did carpentry were carpenters, and it was considered a pretty lowly job. But the Princess loved oak and chestnut and boxwood. She loved sawing it and planing it and making things from it.

Of course, if her father had found out, he'd

have probably jumped through the hole in his crown with rage, because it was such an unprincess-like thing to do. But he never did find out, until . . . well, hang on! That's jumping to the end of the story.

Now the Princess was not only very keen on carpentry, she was also very good at it. So she built herself a flying boat, and attached six white-necked swans to it. Then she stood in the market square, disguised as a lunatic, and called out:

'Who wants to touch the moon?'

Well, of course, she pretty soon had a crowd of people around her, all laughing and making fun of her and pretending they wanted to touch the moon. So she invited them into her flying boat, and they all piled in, still joking and smiling and thinking the Princess was just some poor lunatic.

Then – to everyone's surprise – she cracked her whip, and the swans flew up into the air, pulling the flying boat up with them. Up and up they rose, until they were as high as the moon, and everyone leaned out and touched it. Just like that.

When they returned to the earth, however, they found the King in a terrible rage, surrounded by his guards.

'Arrest that lunatic!' screamed the King.

But the Princess flew above the King and his guards, and called down:

'What's the matter? I thought you wanted to touch the moon. Jump aboard and I'll fly you there!'

But the King screamed with rage. 'There's only one way to touch the moon!' he cried. 'And that's from the battlements of my Tower – standing on tiptoe!'

'But we've already touched it,' cried the citizens, who'd flown in the flying boat. 'Look! You can see our fingermarks all over it!'

The King looked up and he could indeed see their fingermarks all over the moon – like little smudges. (For you must know that up until that time the moon had been just plain white, and had no markings at all.)

'Fly with her!' pleaded all the citizens. 'Touch the moon! And then we can all stop building this wretched Tower that has destroyed our kingdom!'

But the King went purple with rage. 'No one

will stop me building my Tower!' he cried. And he ordered his archers to shoot the six white-necked swans, so the flying boat came crashing down to earth, and the King's Daughter with it.

When the citizens ran to her side, they found her disguise had fallen off, and they recognized the Princess. They turned to the King and said: 'Now see what you've done! You've killed your own daughter!'

Whereupon the King knelt down by her side and grief swept over him like a hand wiping a slate clean. 'I've been mad!' he cried. 'I have been obsessed – not with touching the moon – but with my own power and glory.'

And there and then he ordered his workmen to destroy the Tower, and start to rebuild his kingdom and his people's homes.

At this moment, the Princess stirred – for she had not been killed by the fall, only stunned – and she murmured:

'Why touch the moon? It looks best as it is.'

And from that day on, no one in that land ever thought of touching the moon again.

But, you know, it still has their fingermarks all over it, and, if you look up at it on a clear night, you will see them – like a face crying out: 'Don't touch me!'

TOM AND THE DINOSAUR

A small boy named Tom once noticed noises coming from the old woodshed that stood at the very bottom of his garden. One noise sounded a bit like his Great Aunt Nelly breathing through a megaphone. There was also a sort of scraping, rattling noise, which sounded a bit like someone rubbing several giant tiddlywinks together. There was also a rumbling sort of noise that could have been a very small volcano erupting in a pillarbox. There was also a sort of scratching noise – rather like a mouse the size of a rhinoceros trying not to frighten the cat.

Tom said to himself: 'If I didn't know better, I'd say it all sounded exactly as if we had a dinosaur living in our woodshed.'

So he climbed on to a crate, and looked through the woodshed window – and do you know what he saw?

'My hat!' exclaimed Tom. 'It's a Stegosaurus!'

He was pretty certain about it, and he also knew that although it looked ferocious, that particular dinosaur only ate plants. Nevertheless, just to be on the safe side, he ran to his room, and looked up 'Stegosaurus' in one of his books on dinosaurs.

'I knew I was right!' he said, when he found it. Then he read through the bit about it being a vegetarian, and checked the archaeological evidence for that. It seemed pretty convincing.

'I just hope they're right,' muttered Tom to himself, as he unlocked the door of the woodshed. 'I mean after sixty million years, it would be dead easy to mistake a vegetarian for a flesh-eating monster!'

He opened the door of the woodshed *very* cautiously, and peered in.

The Stegosaurus certainly looked ferocious. It had great bony plates down its back, and vicious spikes on the end of its tail. On the other hand, it didn't look terribly well. Its head was resting on the floor, and a branch with strange leaves and red berries on it was sticking out of its mouth. The rumbling sound (like the volcano in the pillarbox) was coming from its stomach. Occasionally the Stegosaurus burped and groaned slightly.

'It's got indigestion,' said Tom to himself. 'Poor thing!' And he stepped right in and patted the Stegosaurus on the head.

This was a mistake.

The Stegosaurus may have been just a plant-eater, but it was also thirty feet long, and as soon as Tom touched it, it reared up on to its hind legs

– taking most of the woodshed with it.

If the thing had looked pretty frightening when it was lying with its head on the floor, you can imagine how even more terrifying it was when it towered thirty feet above Tom.

'Don't be frightened!' said Tom to the Stegosaurus. 'I won't hurt you.'

The Stegosaurus gave a roar . . . well, actually it wasn't really a roar so much as an extremely loud bleat: 'Baa*a* - baa*a* - baa*a*!' it roared, and fell back on all fours. Tom only just managed to jump out of the way in time, as half the woodshed came crashing down with it, and splintered into pieces around the Stegosaurus. At the same time, the ground shook as the huge creature's head slumped back on to the floor.

Once again, Tom tried to pat it on the head. This time, the Stegosaurus remained where it was, but one lizard-like eye stared at Tom rather hard, and its tummy gave another rumble.

'You must have eaten something that disagreed with you,' said Tom, and he picked up the branch that had been in the dinosaur's mouth.

'I've never seen berries like that before,' said Tom. The Stegosaurus looked at the branch balefully.

'Is this what gave you tummy-ache?' asked Tom.

The Stegosaurus turned away as Tom offered it the branch.

'You don't like it, do you?' said Tom. 'I wonder what they taste like?'

As Tom examined the strange red berries, he thought to himself: 'No one has tasted these berries for sixty million years . . . Probably no human being has *ever* tasted them.'

Somehow the temptation to try one of the berries was overwhelming, but Tom told himself not to be so stupid. If they'd given a huge creature like the Stegosaurus tummy-ache, they could well be deadly to a small animal like Tom. And yet . . . they looked so . . . *tempting* . . . The Stegosaurus gave a low groan and shifted its head so it could look at Tom.

'Well, I wonder how you'd get on with twentieth-century vegetables?' said Tom, pulling up one of his father's turnips. He proffered it to the dinosaur. But the Stegosaurus turned its head away, and then – quite suddenly and for no apparent reason – it bit Tom's other hand.

'Ouch!' exclaimed Tom, and hit the Stegosaurus on the nose with the turnip.

'Baaa!' roared the Stegosaurus, and bit the turnip.

Finding a bit of turnip in its mouth, the Stegosaurus started to chew it. Then suddenly it spat it all out.

'That's the trouble with you dinosaurs,' said Tom. 'You've got to learn to adapt . . . otherwise . . .'

Tom found himself looking at the strange red berries again.

'You see,' Tom began again to the Stegosaurus, 'we human beings are ready to change our habits

... that's why we're so successful ... we'll try different foods ... in fact ... I wonder what fruit from sixty million years ago tastes like? Hey! Stop that!'

The Stegosaurus was butting Tom's arm with its nose.

'You want to try something else?' asked Tom, and he pulled up a parsnip from the vegetable patch. But before he could get back to the Stegosaurus, it had lumbered to its feet and started to munch away at his father's prize rose-bushes.

'Hey! Don't do that! My dad'll go crazy!' shouted Tom. But the Stegosaurus was making short work of the roses. And there was really nothing Tom could do about it.

He hit the Stegosaurus on the leg, but it merely flicked its huge tail, and Tom was lucky to escape as the bony spikes on the end missed him by inches.

'That's a deadly tail you've got there!' exclaimed Tom, and he decided to keep a respectable distance between himself and the monster.

It was at that moment that Tom suddenly did the craziest thing he'd ever done in his life. He couldn't explain later why he'd done it. He just did. He shouldn't have done, but he did ... He pulled off one of the strange red berries and popped it into his mouth.

Now this is something you must never ever do – if you don't know what the berries are – because some berries, like Deadly Nightshade, are *really* poisonous.

But Tom pulled off one of the sixty-million-year-old berries, and ate it. It was very bitter, and he was just about to spit it out, when he noticed something wasn't quite right . . .

The garden was turning round. Tom was standing perfectly still, but the garden . . . indeed, as far as he could see, the whole world . . . was turning around and around, slowly at first, and then faster and faster . . . until the whole world was spinning about him like a whirlwind − faster and faster and faster and everything began to blur together. At the same time there was a roaring noise − as if all the sounds in the world had been jumbled up together − louder and faster and louder until there was a shriek! . . . And everything stopped. And Tom could once again see where he was . . . or, rather, where he wasn't . . . for the first thing he realized was that he was no longer standing in his back garden . . . or, if he was, he couldn't see the remains of the woodshed, nor his father's vegetable patch nor his house. Nor could he see the Stegosaurus.

There was a bubbling pool of hot mud where the rose-bushes should have been. And in place of the house there was a forest of the tallest trees Tom had ever seen. Over to his right, where the Joneses' laundry line had been hanging, there was a steaming jungle swamp.

But to Tom by far the most interesting thing was the thing he found himself standing in. It was a sort of crater scooped out of the ground, and it was ringed with a dozen or so odd-shaped eggs.

'My hat!' said Tom to himself. 'I'm back in Jurassic times! One hundred and fifty million years ago! And, by the look of it, I'm standing right in a dinosaur's nest!'

At that moment he heard an ear-splitting screech, and a huge lizard came running out of the forest on its hind legs. It was heading straight for Tom! Well, Tom didn't wait to ask what time of day it was – he just turned and fled. But once he was running, he realized it was hopeless. He had about as much chance of out-running the lizard creature as he had of teaching it Latin (which, as he didn't even speak it himself, was pretty unlikely).

Tom had run no more than a couple of paces by the time the creature had reached the nest. Tom shut his eyes. The next second he knew he would feel the creature's hooked claws around his neck. But he kept on running . . . and running . . . and nothing happened.

Eventually, Tom turned to see his pursuer had stopped at the nest and was busy with something.

'It's eating the eggs!' exclaimed Tom. 'It's an egg-eater . . . an Oviraptor! I should have recognized it!'

But before he had a chance to kick himself, he felt his feet sinking beneath him, and an uncomfortably hot sensation ran up his legs. Tom looked down to see that he'd run into the bog.

'Help!' shouted Tom. But the Oviraptor obviously knew as little English as it did Latin, and Tom felt his legs sliding deeper into the bubbling mud.

Tom looked up, and saw what looked like flying lizards gliding stiffly overhead. He wished he could grab on to one of those long tails and pull himself up out of the bog, but – even as he thought it – his legs slid in up to the knee. And now he suddenly realized the mud was not just hot – it was *boiling* hot!

His only chance was to grab a nearby fern frond. With his last ounce of strength, Tom lunged for it and managed to grab the end. The fern was tougher and stronger than modern ferns, but it also stung his hand. But he put up with it, and slowly and painfully, inch by inch, he managed to claw his way up the fern frond until he finally managed to pull himself free of the bog.

'This isn't any place for me!' exclaimed Tom, and, at that moment, the sky grew red – as if some distant volcano were erupting.

'Oh dear!' said Tom. 'How on earth do I get out of this?'

The moment he said it, however, he took it back, for the most wonderful thing happened. At least, it was wonderful for Tom, because he was particularly interested in these things.

He heard a terrible commotion in the forest. There was a crashing and roaring and twittering and bleating. A whole flock of Pterodactyls flew up out of the trees with hideous screeching. The lizard creature stopped eating the eggs and turned to look.

From out of the middle of the forest came the most terrible roar that Tom had ever heard in his life. The ground shook. The lizard thing screamed, dropped the egg it was devouring and ran off as fast as it could. Then out of the forest came another dinosaur, followed by another and another and another. Big ones, small ones, some running on four legs, some on two. All looking terrified and screeching and howling.

Tom shinned up a nearby tree to keep out of the way. 'Those are Ankylosaurs! Those are Pterosaurs! Triceratops! Iguanadons! Oh! And look: a Plateosaurus!'

Tom could scarcely believe his luck. 'Imagine seeing so many different kinds of dinosaur all at the same time!' he said to himself.
'I wonder where they're going?'
   But the words were scarcely out of his mouth before he found out.

CRASH! Tom nearly fell out of the tree. CRASH! The ground shook, as suddenly – out of the forest – there emerged the most terrible creature Tom had ever seen or was ever likely to see again.

'Crumbs!' said Tom. 'I should have guessed! Tyrannosaurus Rex! My favourite dinosaur!'

The monster stepped out into the clearing. It was bigger than a house, and it strode on two massive legs. Its vicious teeth glowed red in the flaming light from the sky.

The curious thing was that Tom seemed to forget all his fear. He was so overawed by the sight of the greatest of all dinosaurs that he felt everything else was insignificant – including himself.

The next moment, however, all his fear returned with a vengeance, for the Tyrannosaurus Rex stopped as it drew level with the tree in which Tom was hiding. Its great head loomed just above

Tom and the tree, and made them both quiver like jelly.

Before Tom knew what was happening, he suddenly saw the Tyrannosaurus reach out its foreclaws and pull the tree over towards itself. The next second, Tom found that the branch to which he was clinging had been ripped off the tree, and he was being hoisted forty feet above the ground in the claws of the Tyrannosaurus Rex!

Tom was too terrified to be frightened. A sort of calm hit him as the creature turned him over and sniffed him – as if uncertain as to whether or not Tom was edible.

'He's going to find out pretty soon!' exclaimed Tom, as he felt himself lifted up towards those terrible jaws. 'I bet,' thought Tom, 'I'm the only boy in my school ever to have been eaten by his own favourite dinosaur!'

He could feel the monster's breath on his skin. He could see the glittering eye looking at him. He could sense the jaws were just opening to tear him to pieces, when . . . there was a dull thud.

The Tyrannosaurus's head jerked upright, and it twisted round, and Tom felt himself falling through the air.

The branch broke his fall, and as he picked himself up, he saw that something huge had landed on the Tyrannosaurus's back. The Tyrannosaurus had leapt around in surprise and was now tearing and ripping at the thing that had landed on it.

And now, as Tom gathered his wits, he suddenly realized what it was that had apparently fallen out of nowhere on to the flesh-eating monster. I wonder if you can guess what it was? . . . It was Tom's old friend the Stegosaurus − complete with bits of the garden woodshed still stuck in its armour plates, and the branch of red berries sticking out of its mouth.

'It must have given up eating my dad's roses and gone back to the berries!' exclaimed Tom. And, at that very moment, Tom could have kicked himself. 'I'm an idiot!' he cried. For he suddenly noticed that the tree he'd climbed was none other than the very same magical tree − with its odd-shaped leaves and bright red berries.

But even as he reached out his hand to pick a berry that would send him back again in time, he found himself hurtling through the air, as the Tyrannosaurus's tail struck him on the back.

'Baaa!' bleated the Stegosaurus, as the Tyrannosaurus clawed its side and blood poured onto the ground.

'R**aaaa**!' roared the Tyrannosaurus as the Stegosaurus thrashed it with the horny spikes on its tail.

The monsters reared up on their hind legs, and fought with tooth and bone and claw, and they swayed and teetered high above Tom's head, until the Tyrannosaurus lunged with its savage jaws, and ripped a huge piece of flesh from the Stegosaurus's side. The Stegosaurus began to topple . . . as if in slow motion . . . directly on to where Tom was crouching.

And Tom would most certainly have been crushed beneath the creature, had he not – at that very instant – found that in his hand he already had a broken spray of the red berries. And as the monster toppled over on to him, he popped a berry into his mouth and bit it.

Once again the world began to spin around him. The clashing dinosaurs, the forest, the bubbling mud swamp, the fiery sky – all whirled around him in a crescendo of noise and then . . . suddenly! . . . there he was back in his own garden. The Joneses' washing was still on the line. There was his house, and there was his father coming down the garden path towards him looking none too pleased.

'Dad!' yelled Tom. 'You'll never guess what's just happened!'

Tom's father looked at the wrecked woodshed, and the dug-up vegetable patch and then he looked at his prize roses scattered all over the garden. Then he looked at Tom:

'No, my lad,' he said, 'I don't suppose I can. But I'll tell you this . . . It had better be a *very* good story!'

NOTE: If you're wondering why the magical tree with the bright red berries has never been heard of again, well, the Stegosaurus landed on it and smashed it, and I'm afraid it was the only one of its kind.

Oh! What happened to the Stegosaurus? Well, I'm happy to be able to tell you that it actually won its fight against the Tyrannosaurus Rex. It was, in fact, the only time a Stegosaurus ever beat a Tyrannosaurus. This is mainly due to the fact that this particular Tyrannosaurus suddenly got a terrible feeling of *déjà-vu* and had to run off and find its mummy for reassurance (because it was only a young Tyrannosaurus Rex after all). So the Stegosaurus went on to become the father of six healthy young Stegosauruses or Stegosauri, and Jurassic Tail-Thrashing Champion of what is now Surbiton!

This is the story of the most extraordinary child who ever stuck his tongue out at the Prime Minister. His name was Nicobobinus [*Nick-Oh-Bob-In-Us*]. He lived a long time ago, in a city called Venice, and he could do anything.

Of course, not everybody knew he could do anything. In fact only his best friend, Rosie, knew he could, and nobody took any notice of anything Rosie said, because she was always having wild ideas anyway.

One day, for example, Rosie said to Nicobobinus: 'Let's put a rabbit down the Doge's trousers!'

'Don't be silly,' said Nicobobinus. 'The Doge doesn't wear trousers.'

'Yes he does,' said Rosie. '*And* we ought to boil his hat up and give it to the pigeons.'

'Anyway, who *is* the Doge?' asked Nicobobinus.

'How d'you know he doesn't wear trousers if

you don't know who he is?' exclaimed Rosie (not unreasonably in my opinion).

Nicobobinus peered across the water and muttered: 'He doesn't live in the Doge's palace, does he?'

'Gosh!' said Rosie. 'I've never been fishing with a real genius before.'

'But he's the most important man in Venice!' exclaimed Nicobobinus.

'They've got universities for people like you, you know,' said Rosie, and she yanked a small carp out of the canal.

'What have you got against him?' asked Nicobobinus, as he watched her pulling out the hook with a well-practised twist.

'He's just extended his palace,' said Rosie, looking at her fish. It was about twenty-three centimetres long.

'So?' said Nicobobinus, wondering why *he* never caught anything longer than his nose – which wasn't particularly long anyway.

'Well, he extended it all over my granny's house. That's what!' said Rosie.

'And now your poor old gran hasn't got anywhere to live?' asked Nicobobinus sympathetically.

'Oh yes she has! She's living with us, and I can't stand it!' replied Rosie.

Nicobobinus pretended, for a moment, that *he* had a bite. Then he said: 'But how will putting a rabbit down the Doge's trousers help?'

'It won't,' said Rosie. 'But it'll make me feel a lot better. Come on!'

'You don't really mean it?' gasped Nicobobinus.

'No,' said Rosie. 'We haven't got a rabbit – so it'll have to be a fish.'

'But that's our supper!' said Nicobobinus. 'And anyway, they've got guards and sentries and dogs all over the Doge's palace. We'd never get in.'

Rosie looked Nicobobinus straight in the eyes and said: 'Nicobobinus! It's *fun!*'

Some time later, when they were hiding under some nets on one of the little fishing boats that ferried people from the Giudecca to St Mark's Square, when the weather was too bad for fishing, Nicobobinus was still less certain.

'My granny says that where her kitchen used to be, they've built this fancy balcony,' Rosie was whispering, 'and she reckons any thief could climb in by day or night.'

'They drown thieves in the Grand Canal at midnight,' groaned Nicobobinus.

'They'll never catch us,' Rosie reassured him.

'Who's that under my nets?' shouted a voice.

'Leg it!' yelled Rosie, and she and Nicobobinus jumped overboard!

'Lucky we'd reached the shore!' panted Nicobobinus as the two sprinted across St Mark's Square.

'Hey! You two!' yelled the fisherman and gave chase.

Some time later, as Nicobobinus was standing on Rosie's shoulders pulling himself on to the balcony of the Doge's palace, he was even less certain.

'Have you got the fish?' hissed Rosie, as he pulled her up after him.

Nicobobinus could feel it wriggling inside his jerkin.

'No,' he replied. 'It was so unhappy I set it free.

It said it didn't want to get caught by the Doge's guards in the company of two completely out-of-their-basket idiots like . . .

'Look!' said Rosie. 'Do you see where we are?'

Nicobobinus peered into the room with Rosie and caught his breath. It was a magnificent room, with lacquered gold furniture and elegant paintings on the wall. But that wasn't what caught the attention of Rosie and Nicobobinus.

'Do you see?' exclaimed Rosie.

'Toys!' breathed Nicobobinus.

'We're in the nursery!' said Rosie, and she was. She had just climbed in.

Back at home Nicobobinus had just one toy. His uncle had made it for him, and, now he came to think about it, it was more of a plank than a toy. It had four wooden wheels, but the main part of it was definitely a plank. Rosie thought about her two toys, back in the little bare room where she slept with her sisters and her mother and her father and now her granny. One was moth-eaten (that was the doll that had been handed down from sister to sister) and the other was broken (that was a jug that she used to pretend was a crock of gold). But the Doge's children had: hoops, spinning tops, hobby horses, doll's houses, dolls, toy furniture, masks, windmills, stilts (of various heights), rattles, building blocks, boxes, balls and a swing.

'There's only one thing,' whispered Rosie.

'What's that?' asked Nicobobinus as he picked up one of the hoops.

'The Doge hasn't got any children,' said Rosie, but before she could say anything else, one of them walked in through the door.

'Hasn't he?' said Nicobobinus.

'Well I didn't think he had,' said Rosie.

During this last exchange, the little girl who had just walked in through the door had turned pale, turned on her heel, and finally turned into a human cannonball, that streaked off back the way it had come.

'Quick!' cried Rosie. 'She'll give the alarm!'

And before Nicobobinus could stop her, Rosie was off in pursuit. So Nicobobinus followed ... What else could he do?

Well, they hadn't got more than half-way across the adjoining room, when they both noticed it was rather full of people.

'Hi, everyone!' yelled Nicobobinus, because he couldn't think of anything else to say.

'That's torn it!' muttered Rosie. And on they dashed into the next chamber.

The Doge, who had been one of the people the room was full of, sat up in bed and said: 'Who are *they*?'

'I'll have them executed straightaway,' said the Prime Minister.

'No, no! *Apprehend* them,' said the Doge.

'At once,' said the Chief of the Guards.

'My clothes!' said the Doge, and sixteen people rushed forward with sixteen different bits of the Doge's clothing. Getting out of bed for the Most Important Person In Venice in 1545 was a lot more elaborate than it is for you or me ... at least, it's more elaborate than the way I get up – I don't really know about you ...

Anyway, by this time, Nicobobinus and Rosie had bolted through six more rooms, down a flight of stairs and locked themselves in a cupboard.

'Phew!' said Rosie. 'Sorry about this.'

'That's all right,' said Nicobobinus.

'Please don't hurt me,' said a third voice. Nicobobinus and Rosie looked at each other in astonishment (although, as it was pitch-dark in the cupboard, neither of them realized they did).

'Who's that?' asked Nicobobinus.

'I'm not allowed to play with other children,' said the voice. 'My nurse says they might hurt me or kidnap me.'

'Don't be daft!' exclaimed Rosie. 'Children don't kidnap other children.'

'Don't they?' said the other occupant of the cupboard.

'No. And _we're_ not going to hurt you,' said Nicobobinus.

'Then why are you here?'

'A lark,' said Rosie.

'What's that?' asked the girl.

'You know ...' said Nicobobinus, 'fun.'

'Fun?' said the little girl. 'What's that?'

'Oh dear,' muttered Rosie.

'Stick with us and you'll see,' said Nicobobinus.

'All right,' said the girl. 'My name's Beatrice.'

But before either Nicobobinus or Rosie could tell Beatrice their names, there was a thundering as dozens of people went storming and clattering past the cupboard shouting things like: 'There they are!' and 'No! That's not them!' and 'Ow! Take that spear out of my ear!' and 'Quick! This way!' and 'Look in there!' and 'Help me! I've fallen over!' and so on.

When they'd all finally gone and it was quiet again, Nicobobinus, Rosie and their new friend stuck their heads out of the cupboard. The coast was clear, except for the guard who had fallen over.

'Give me a hand, would you?' he asked. 'This armour's so heavy that once you fall over it's very difficult to get back on your feet again.'

'Doesn't that make it rather hard to fight in?' said Nicobobinus as they helped him to stand upright.

'Hopeless,' admitted the guard. 'But it *is* very expensive. Now, have you seen two children go past here?'

'Yes,' said Beatrice. 'They went that way!'

'Thanks!' said the guard and ran off as fast as his expensive armour would allow him. He'd got round the corner before he must have realized he'd made a mistake, for there was a crash and a muffled curse as he tried to stop and turn, but fell over again instead.

'Come on!' yelled Rosie.

'Is this fun?' asked Beatrice, as they ran up another staircase and on to a long balcony and looked out over a narrow street.

'Are you enjoying it?' asked Nicobobinus.

'So-so,' said Beatrice.

'Then it's probably fun,' said Nicobobinus.

'Oh! Stop wittering, you two!' exclaimed Rosie. 'And help me down off here!' Rosie was already climbing over the balustrade and hanging from the balcony.

'That's too far a drop!' exclaimed Beatrice.

'You wait!' grinned Nicobobinus. 'We've done this before.' He whipped his belt off, and before you could say 'Venice and chips!' Rosie was clinging to the end, and being lowered down into the street.

'Oo-er!' said Beatrice.

'Come on!' called Rosie.

'Are you sure this is fun?' whispered Beatrice.

'Well it beats enjoying yourself!' shouted Nicobobinus, as several guards suddenly appeared at the far end of the balcony.

'Hurry!' he said, and thrust the end of the belt into her hand.

'There they are!' shouted one of the guards. And without giving another thought, Beatrice followed Rosie down into the street.

'Nicobobinus!' yelled Rosie. 'How are you going to get down?'

'I'll be OK!' yelled Nicobobinus, although his

main thought, as he ducked through a window, was actually 'Cripes!'

'I thought you'd done this before?' said Beatrice as she and Rosie legged it down the street.

'Well ... maybe not from quite such a high balcony,' admitted Rosie, and they disappeared round the corner.

Nicobobinus meanwhile had made a discovery. He had discovered that the window that looked out on to the long balcony that looked over the Calle de San Marco was the window of the office of the Prime Minister. He also made a second discovery: it was office hours. The Prime Minister was sitting on a sort of throne, holding an audience with several rather scruffy individuals who looked scared out of their wits.

'... and then take their heads off,' the Prime Minister was saying, as Nicobobinus backed in through the window and landed in front of him. 'Ah!' smiled the Prime Minister, signalling to his guards, 'another customer.'

Some time later, Nicobobinus found himself chained and shackled and being dragged into the Grand Audience Chamber of the Doge of Venice himself. It was a particularly magnificent room, and nowadays people come from all over the world to gaze up at the ornate ceiling and stare at the fine furnishings, while a guide talks too quickly in a language they can't understand and tells them about all the boring and pompous men and women with famous names that have come and gone through the doors of that famous place. But one story they never tell (and I don't know why) is the story I'm telling you now.

At that particular moment, however, the one thing Nicobobinus was *not* interested in was the magnificent decor of the Grand Audience Chamber. His one and only concern was how to get out again as quickly as possible (which, come to think of it, is probably what most of today's tourists are thinking too!).

'Bring the boy here,' yawned the Doge (who was actually wishing he was back in bed).

'We could start by simply cutting his feet off, and then move on up to his knees . . .' the Prime Minister was whispering in the Doge's ear as Nicobobinus was thrown on to the floor in front of them.

All eyes were upon him, and an excited buzz went around the Audience Chamber. The Doge looked at him and then said: 'What are your demands?'

Nicobobinus thought he hadn't heard right, so

he said: 'I beg your pardon, Your Highness?'

'Where is she?' shrieked the Prime Minister, and suddenly everyone in the room was muttering and shouting the same thing.

'Silence!' commanded the Doge. Then he turned to Nicobobinus once more and said: 'You have kidnapped my daughter. I will give you what you want, providing you return her at once – unharmed.'

Nicobobinus was just about to say: 'No! I *haven't* kidnapped your daughter', but he didn't. Instead, he looked around at all the heavy, brooding faces, the wine-soaked noses and the sunken eyes of all the important, pompous folk of Venice, and he said: 'I want one thing.'

'Yes?' said the Doge.

'And it isn't for me,' went on Nicobobinus.

'It's for your master,' assumed the Doge.

'No,' replied Nicobobinus, 'it's for your daughter.' A gasp went up around the room. 'It's something you must give Beatrice.'

The Doge couldn't speak for a moment, but eventually he managed to say:

'And what is it?'

'Fun,' said Nicobobinus.

'Fun?' said the Doge.

'Fun?' said all the pompous and important people of Venice.

'Fun!' said another voice, and there was Beatrice, the Doge's daughter, standing at the entrance to the Grand Audience Chamber, holding Rosie's hand. 'We've been having fun!'

Well, to cut a long story short, the Prime Minister still wanted to chop off Nicobobinus's and Rosie's heads and drown them in the Grand Canal at midnight, until the Lord Chief Advocate pointed out (after consulting various medical authorities) that you can't drown someone once you've cut their head off.

'Then just drown them like the rats they are!' exclaimed the Prime Minister.

'But they're only children,' said the Doge's mother.

'That's beside the point!' screamed the Prime Minister. 'It's the *principle* that matters! If you don't drown them, soon you'll have all the riff-raff of Venice climbing into the palace and making demands!'

But the Doge had fallen asleep, and his mother ordered that Beatrice should decide what was to become of Nicobobinus and Rosie. Beatrice said they had to come and play with her every Monday. And so that was that.

Later that evening, as the Doge was getting into bed, and all the assistants were gone, he said to his wife: 'You know, my dear, a most extraordinary thing . . . Just now . . . Do you know what I found in my trousers?'

At about the same time, Nicobobinus and Rosie were sitting on Nicobobinus's doorstep laughing and laughing as Nicobobinus described how he had managed to slip the wriggling fish past the Doge's belt and into his trousers while the Doge's mother was kissing him goodnight.

'But one thing puzzles me,' said Rosie. 'When did you stick your tongue out at the Prime Minister?'

'I didn't,' replied Nicobobinus. 'That happened in a totally different adventure.'

'Was it the one where we set off to find the Land of the Dragons?' asked Rosie.

'Ah!' said Nicobobinus. '*That* would be telling . . .'

Some other books by Terry Jones in Puffin

FAIRY TALES

**Stories of magic, adventure and imagination –
Terry Jones's *Fairy Tales* make thrilling
reading.**

'Terry Jones is a gifted storyteller . . . perfect
for reading aloud'
– *Good Book Guide To Children's Books*

'Here is an author setting out to rival the classic
fairy tales and making an exciting job of it'
– Rachel Billington in the *Financial Times*

' . . . could conceivably become a "modern
classic" . . . the book is a joy'
– Brian Patten in the *Spectator*

NICOBOBINUS

This is the story of the most amazing, extraordinary child who ever stuck his tongue out at the Prime Minister. His name was Nicobobinus. He lived a long time ago in Venice and he could do anything.

'Terry Jones combines fairy story, adventure, magic, mystery and humour with apparently effortless skill. The result is captivating'
– *Children's Books of the Year*

'Terry Jones is undoubtedly one of the most consistently entertaining writers for children'
– *Books for Your Children*

'New fairy tales are a rare occurrence . . . this one enthrals like the best of the old stories. Here are thirty-one chapters of suspense . . .'
– *Sunday Times*

'Fantasy, adventure and morality are perfectly mixed in this funny, fast-moving story. A marvellous book'
– *The Good Book Guide to Children's Books*

'Terry Jones's splendid children's comic fantasy adventure story' – *Independent*

'an utterly splendid yarn' – *Observer*

The Saga of Erik the Viking

**This is one tale of a Viking warrior who lived
hundreds and hundreds of years ago.
His name was Erik.**

And Erik was no ordinary Viking. With his
trusty band of men he sets sail in search of
the land where the sun goes at night. In fact, he
finds much more! The Sea Dragon, the Old
Man of the Sea, Dogfighters and giants
combine to make his voyage a great saga of
thrilling adventures.

Winner of the Children's Book Award

READ MORE IN PUFFIN

For children of all ages, Puffin represents quality and variety – the very best in publishing today around the world.

For complete information about books available from Puffin – and Penguin – and how to order them, contact us at the appropriate address below. Please note that for copyright reasons the selection of books varies from country to country.

On the worldwide web: www.penguin.co.uk

In the United Kingdom: Please write to *Dept. EP, Penguin Books Ltd, Bath Road, Harmondsworth, West Drayton, Middlesex UB7 ODA*

In the United States: Please write to *Penguin Putnam inc., P.O. Box 12289, Dept B, Newark, New Jersey 07101-5289* or call 1-800-788-6262.

In Canada: Please write to *Penguin Books Canada Ltd, 10 Alcorn Avenue, Suite 300, Toronto, Ontario M4V 3B2*

In Australia: Please write to *Penguin Books Australia Ltd, P.O. Box 257, Ringwood, Victoria 3134*

In New Zealand: Please write to *Penguin Books (NZ) Ltd, Private Bag 102902, North Shore Mail Centre, Auckland 10*

In India: Please write to *Penguin Books India Pvt Ltd, 11 Panscheel Shopping Centre, Panscheel Park, New Delhi 110 017*

In the Netherlands: Please write to *Penguin Books Netherlands bv, Postbus 3507, NL-1001 AH Amsterdam*

In Germany: Please write to *Penguin Books Deutschland GmbH, Metzlerstrasse 26, 60594 Frankfurt am Main*

In Spain: Please write to *Penguin Books S. A., Bravo Murillo 19, 1° B, 28015 Madrid*

In Italy: Please write to *Penguin Italia s.r.l., Via Felice Casati 20, I–20124 Milano*

In France: Please write to *Penguin France S. A., 17 rue Lejeune, F–31000 Toulouse*

In Japan: Please write to *Penguin Books Japan, Ishikiribashi Building, 2–5–4, Suido, Bunkyo-ku, Tokyo 112*

In South Africa: Please write to *Longman Penguin Southern Africa (Pty) Ltd, Private Bag X08, Bertsham 2013*